FIERCE LIKE AN OAK TREE

FIERCE LIKE AN OAK TREE

A Collection of Short Stories
Rooted in Sharp, Louisiana

Rae Cupples Champagne, PhD

Edited by Rose Talbot Brumley
Cover design by Katie Callow

ISBN: 979-8-218-51746-5
Published by Westbrae Literary Group
Berkeley, California
Jon-David Hague, Founding Editor

For more information about this and other titles from Westbrae Literary Group, visit us at westbraeliterarygroup.com or email us at info@westbraeliterarygroup.com

For Raym.

CONTENTS

Preface

At first glance, this might seem like a simple collection of stories to pick up and read at random, but in essence, it's an episodic novel—one story thread woven together through episodes or *moments*. The narrator remains constant, and as her life unfolds, so does her voice, which matures along the way. I chose not to label this as an episodic novel because that felt grandiose, somehow making the content less approachable. I only bring the term up now to emphasize that the stories are interrelated. While many can stand alone, they mean more when the unifying elements are connected, such as the large oaks referenced in both the beginning and the end.

My intended audience was originally quite small— the families of Sharp, or at least those aware of it—as this project was a way to honor the community my dad loved so much. Yet, as I revised the pieces for publication, I found myself gradually reshaping them to reflect the narrator's journey of coming to terms with her faith-based heritage at different stages of life. It's a universal theme that should resonate with anyone who grew up in a close-knit Southern community within the Bible Belt.

In the safety of these pages, I am able to speak with surety and, often, with brutal honesty. A friend who read an early version commented that my "voice" in the title piece, "Fierce Like an Oak Tree," is especially vulnerable and raw. This made my effort feel worthwhile, as my highest aim is to be authentic.

One of the most difficult tasks has been to avoid predictability, as I love stories that offer some sort of revelation. To that end, I've tried to embody the voice of an inarticulate questioner, always seeking, always figuring things out. This curiosity, paired with my affection for good-natured pokes at Southern eccentricities, shaped the way I approached the narrative. While these peculiarities are not my main focus (and I'll admit, I get irritated when authors overdo stereotypes), I couldn't resist incorporating a few. Finally, in the true Southern gothic way, death has found its way into nearly every story. What surprised me most, though, is that joy appears to shine through every instance of death. Perhaps my own biggest takeaway from working through this project has been realizing a unique view of death. My perspective is absurd, but consistently soft and full of assurance.

I want to make it clear that no part of this fictional work should be taken as exact history, biography, or autobiography. By weaving in elements from past experiences, my intent is to highlight the eternality of living—to showcase, as William Faulkner has famously said, "there is no such thing as *was*." So, while some names are real, others are not. Some dates are accurate, and some are skewed purposefully. Only the seeds of the stories are true, and just like seeds planted and forgotten, these stories are the burgeoning first blooms of deeply-held memories or questions of which I'm only now finding the words.

In the end, this is only a sampling. Many more volumes could be written to convey the quiet but relentless strength of those raised in a good Southern community (the fierce strength of an enduring oak tree). Writing these stories has been a bittersweet journey for me, and, having followed the narrator through a series of events and insights spanning 50 years, I recognize it's time to pause and allow others to carry these threads forward. There is much more to tell and other voices to do so.

It's true that some people spend their adult lives searching for healing from their childhood. I've found that I look back to my childhood when I need healing from my adult life. If you grew up in a community like Sharp, or anywhere that is innately familiar, then *surely you know what I mean.*

Many thanks for picking up this odd little volume. I hope you find something within these pages that you can relate to, and that it makes you smile.

Rae Cupples Champagne
September 2024

I see something of God every hour of the twenty-four,
    and each moment then,
In the faces of men and women I see God, and in my
    own face in the glass . . .

        — Walt Whitman, from *Song of Myself*

ONE

Light of Mine

(2024)

To begin, then, I should probably mention that I'm a bit weird. Well . . . not *weird* in the usual sense. I don't do embarrassing things in public. But my thoughts connect in ways that others might find peculiar. Or maybe I just overthink.

I'll admit that right from the start.

Like many people, when I think of home, there's a nostalgic picture in my mind. But unlike most, in my picture, there's always light—constant and sure, guiding everything to where it belongs.

It's not just any light. Jesus is there.

Well . . . not *Jesus* in the usual imagining with the shoulder-length brown hair and all. He's not visibly there, but there's a warm, peaceful presence.

And I'm a figure in a divine story much bigger than me.

I am from Sharp, Louisiana. Population: 1,469. It's one of the least known communities in the state, an area originally named Castor settled by Scottish-Irish pioneers in the early 1800s, loggers and farmers with a few preachers mixed in. They moved over the Appalachians and on into the South, eventually migrating to the Sabine Territory (an area tucked between Texas and Louisiana) following the Revolutionary War. After founding a rural post office in 1907, they established their families along a 10-mile stretch of Highway 8 from nearby Flatwoods to where it intersects with Highway 1—a swath that's very much a part of me.

Boyce lies six miles to the east, while Alexandria, the nearest "city," is 22 miles in the same direction, just a smidge to the south. The full expanse of Highway 8 stretches 156 miles through five parishes: Vernon, Rapides, Grant, LaSalle, and Catahoula, all agrarian territory beginning on the east side of the Sabine.

In 1975, Central Louisiana Electric Company (CLECO) stepped in, flooding a large belt of land on both sides of Highway 8 and constructing an imposing power plant with a gated entrance. The establishment of Rodemacher Unit 1 effectively created CLECO Lake for all who live here, even if that name never officially made it to a map.

The plant overtly reminded us of its purpose by illuminating the night sky—a beam clearly visible on into Boyce, maybe not all the way to Randy's Grocery or Kile's Jewelry on Ulster, but at least at the Plantation Belle, the diner and truck stop on the way in. Over time, *"He works at CLECO"* became a whispered phrase that stirred up envy among the locals.

Maybe that's how it started—this idea I had that opportunity was something measured by how far that beam stretched.

And by who could see it.

Bright as it was, the beam couldn't touch everything. There were pockets where it didn't quite reach, where the shadows held firm.

Like Aunt Ivy's porch, where she rocked back and forth humming a quiet tune, snapping string beans into a metal washbasin. A widow in her 80s, Iva Beebe was everyone's "Aunt Ivy," and grown men and women playfully fought over her teacakes, a recipe no one could get just right.

Or the Sharp Store, with its old-fashioned gas pumps and insistent jangling bell to notify the shopkeeper of an occasional customer. Tucked in a curve just past the green road sign that marked the border of the community, it remained outside the beam too.

Me? You may be wondering. I grew up with that glow always on the horizon. I was scared of losing sight of it, but, all the while, my eyes were fixed on something much further in the distance.

My preteen years were especially pivotal.

I carried out stacks up to my nose of *Nancy Drews* and *Hardy Boys* from the Book Mobile that came every two weeks. With each case the teenage sleuths cracked, I imagined the thrill of fantastic expeditions. I read each series in order unless Ms. Janie, the traveling librarian, forgot and inadvertently checked the next book out to someone else. On long summer days, I devoured a book per day, envying Nancy Drew for the daring way she explored beyond River Heights.

I read voraciously, with tired eyes lured by far-off mysteries.

And with every story, I felt a persistent ache. A longing I couldn't quite name. An invisible scale hovered in my mind, constantly weighing the comforts of home against the exploits I envisioned. It was a tension that drifted into all aspects of my life, even in the simplest things.

Like our Saturday trips to Big Rocky, the unmapped, out-of-the way swimming hole, for instance.

There, the sunshine filtered through the trees and danced on the surface of the water, hinting that there was something just hidden from view. Big Rocky embodied the same pull between the familiar and the unknown.

So it makes sense that my mental pictures of home are most vivid when I remember the Saturdays Dad would drive us out to Big Rocky in his 1929 Model A. The clunky charm of that old car heightened the sense of adventure. We'd ramble down the narrow Lena-Flatwoods Road, look for the secret identifiers, park in the tall grass, step high to tromp down briers that would catch bare legs, and head off into the woods, searching for the elusive footpath. It was easy to lose the way, and it often took several attempts to trek through the woods just right.

But leaving Big Rocky? That was a whole different thing. The drive back wasn't about *finding* the way; it was about *remembering* it. Each turn and landmark became part of the eternal map we carried within us.

Dad made specific stops on our return trip that were inherent parts of his special ritual. The Sharp Store for orange push-ups, then back onto Highway 8. We'd pass the Sharp United Pentecostal Church on the left, and Beebe Lane. After a good curve, on the right, was Floyd and Louvenia Knight's white frame house, with Leroy Knight's house nestled behind it off at an angle.

Next, mature pine trees created an enchanting tunnel over the road, a canopy of green that transformed into a kaleidoscope of shifting hues as the sun dipped low. The road was straight for a stretch then, with a wide open hay field on the left. Duane "Groovy" and Freida Sharp's house was just barely visible in the distance.

And soon, the final destination.

Dad would take that left turn, puttering two miles down the one-lane gravel road, ending our drive at Campbell Creek Cemetery.

The routine was immutable. Big Rocky. Sharp Store. Campbell Creek Cemetery. Always unhurried and deliberate, as if to etch each into my mind. But no matter how many times we made that last turn, something about stopping at the cemetery never felt routine.

Once, when we had slowly rolled to a stop near the cemetery gate, I leaned forward, peering at the many rows of graves, some well-tended and others nearly hidden beneath overgrowth, indicating the passage of time.

"Dad, why do we always stop here?" I asked, my voice quiet, in reverence to the stillness around me.

He didn't answer right away, just kept his hands on the steering wheel, his eyes fixed on the fuchsia azaleas clustered along the fence line.

"Because," he finally said, his voice low, "we need to remember. Everyone here is part of something bigger."

I frowned, not quite understanding. "But we're alive, Dad. They're just . . . gone."

He turned to me then, his gaze serious but gentle.

"And one day, after I'm gone, you'll come here, and you'll remember too. They've all had their stories. Remembering them helps us see where we fit in."

I looked out at the cemetery again, the memorials standing like silent witnesses, and something in me irrevocably shifted. The weight of Dad's words settled into a corner of my heart that would hold onto them long after the drive was over.

"Okay," I whispered, more to myself than to him.

We sat there in the Model A, finishing our push-ups, not saying much, just looking out at the headstones, and I felt the gravity of all that had come before me.

Later that night, lying in bed, I thought about the cemetery. It felt like a meeting point between the past and present. I considered the lives behind those names etched in stone. Each one had a story. Each one added to the community and, somehow, to me.

Those intentional drives made me see things the way he did. The landmarks and rituals weren't just places or habits. They were like wayposts. They might not have burned as bright as CLECO's lights, but they shone steady enough.

What I didn't realize then was that all of it—the distant glow of the plant, the sunlight through the trees, the slow cadence of Dad's drives—was a reflection of something greater I'd sensed but never fully grasped.

Sharp wasn't just a place. It was a compass, pointing me somewhere far beyond. Well . . . not *too far*, I just live in Texas. But now I can see that the lights of home were always pointing to a warm presence, reflecting the greater light that had been with me all along and had carried me through so much. Even cancer.

I'm ready to share the stories I've held close all these years, to let them shine in their own way, as part of something bigger.

And Dad's gone now. So, I guess it's on me to tell them. I guess it's time.

I'll start at the beginning . . .

What do you think has become of the young and
    old men?
And what do you think has become of the women
    and children?

They are alive and well somewhere,
The smallest sprout shows there is really no death,
And if ever there was it led forward life, and does not
    wait at the end to arrest it . . .

All goes onward and outward, nothing collapses,
And to die is different from what any one supposed,
    and luckier.

—Walt Whitman, from Song of Myself

TWO

Tree, Wood, Cross

(1980)

I am in the front yard twisting in the flat-bottom swing, crossing the chains above my head into an uneven *X*. The paint on the swing has been chipping for several years now, and I can see the silver seat shining through between my legs, mixed in blotches with the yellow of the top layer of paint and the red from many years before. I often wonder who chose that original red and who applied the paint—who mourned as it was scratched away in streaks, like lashes stripping something sacred, leaving only bare metal beneath.

Staring through the heavy, rusted cross, I look up into the mighty oak that allows the swing's chains to wrap its limb, even cradles and swaddles them though they painfully tear through years of layers of growth. The tree protects me, holds me the way it must've held the others who swung beneath it, those who grew up and left.

I wonder, *Where did they go?* There were 9-year-old tomboys with paint-flaked clothes before me. *Where did they all go?* I think about how their laughter must have danced in the air above me, whispering secrets I wish I could hear.

With my bare feet dragging in the dirt, I turn in time to see the first car of the procession pass. I had just begun to unwind the swing, a circular movement that, in tandem, allows me to follow the regal black hearse as it passes in front of my house. I begin the second circle as, painstakingly, another hearse passes.

And then another circle.

Another black hearse.

And then again . . .

I know that there are five hearses in all because my swing will only wind five times before the twist is too tight to hold steady for long. Then, comes the moment to let go, enjoying the effortless free-spinning. As I spin, I usually lean back in a deep arc, checking my hair's slow crawl to the ground. I've waited for it to grow, and I use the chains and the cross as my measuring stick, making sure to brace myself with my hands in the exact same spot every day. Though my palms are always stained with rust and my clothes speckled with red and yellow flakes, I have always trusted my tree.

But now . . . it feels strange, being caught there like that. Should I wave? Stand up? Go inside? Walking toward the house with my back turned seems highly inappropriate.

Stilling the swing, I fold my hands into my lap, sit up straight, and wait. There are 126 cars.

The story in the *Town Talk* explains that the tragedy had occurred at approximately 2 a.m. when Dub Quincy, his wife Judy, their son Truitt (16), their daughters

Farrah and Jess (13 and 11), and their beagle Enoch (just 10 weeks) were sleeping. Their mobile home burned to the ground right next to a large woodpile that was left uncharred. The whole family was caught up in a tornado of fire that touched down right on top of them and then picked up and moved on.

The story, summarizing each life, honed in on the irony that Dub cut and sold firewood for a living. In fact, he was quite known for wood, known for small splinters in his hands and the crosses he whittled, working any leftover, useless branches into decorative pieces, keepsakes for parents noting the name and birth date of each child.

And he was even known for grave markers.

He had quite a stockpile of them. The community depended upon Dub to provide one of his hand-carved crosses until a formal gravestone could be erected.

My thoughts drift to Farrah and Jess (Truitt was, after all, a boy). Did they have a swing? Were their palms rust-stained? Is their puppy, Enoch, where they are now? *Where did they go?*

The story explained that there wasn't money for *interment,* so the funeral home benevolently provided everything for a graveside service, and the board of the cemetery unanimously voted to donate the burial plots. It was the largest funeral the Sharp Community had ever seen, with cars lining both sides of the gravel road that winds quietly to Campbell Creek Cemetery. Multiple funeral canopies were erected side by side to cover the aligned row of caskets, and a throng of people packed in, filling every space.

It happened to be Good Friday, and a community member who was interviewed commented that it was nice the dogwoods were in bloom. Amid the sorrow, the blossoms seemed to whisper of renewal and hope.

The reporter concluded by repeating the final words of the Baptist preacher's eulogy, reminding readers, *We are all God's children. We believe Jesus died on the cross and rose again for our salvation, and we enter into His kingdom when we depart this life.*

On Easter Sunday, I am swinging my legs from the pew when our pastor mentions the Quincys' tragedy in his sermon. He likens the trailer fire to the atoning fire of the Holy Ghost.

I think of Dub's woodpile that was left untouched. I picture neat rows of split pine snugged into one another in perfect triangles with splinters poking out in places and kindling packed in tight between the sticks of wood. I can't imagine someone cutting down my tree, but I understand that trees serve a purpose. After all, they are what provided for Dub and his family. I am grateful that the cut wood is, at least, still cherished.

But I can't get it out of my head why they all died. It's a tragedy, like the preacher said.

The room feels heavy, and I shift in my seat, trying to catch a glimpse through the window at the end of the aisle, hoping for a bit of light to break through.

As the sermon continues, I am thinking of the five uniform mounds, still softly heaped. I imagine being at the cemetery where I can squat down eye level, root my fingers in the dirt, tilt my head just so, and peer down the row of kindred crosses.

Though I am still sitting on the church pew, with a squint to create just the right angle, I feel my sight change to vision as, from my vantage point, the repeating self-made grave markers form a perfect line that ascends into the horizon and appears to extend forever.

I remember the strong arm of the oak that holds my swing then. I fancy myself untwisting the chains, throwing my head back and smiling when my hair finally streams to the ground.

Envisioning the cemetery full of simple wooden crosses, all I see are little trees.

It is you talking just as much as myself, I act as the
    tongue of you,
Tied in your mouth, in mine it begins to be loosened.

—Walt Whitman, from *Song of Myself*

THREE

By Any Other Name

(1981)

When I finally do make it to church, I find Sister Diane there with one hand on her hip and a clipboard directing the full congregation on the particulars of the morning's Easter egg hunt. They are gathered outside in the grassy clearing between the parsonage and the side door to the all-purpose room where the older church ladies quilt on Tuesday mornings.

"Don't *you* look sweet this morning, Missy," she purrs, spotting me as I'm just getting out of the car and walking up. I have on a frilly, yellow flowery-print dress, white bobby socks, and penny loafers—an outfit that wordlessly explains why we are late.

"You know," she says, "Seeing you, I'm thinking that maybe we should set some parameters for the hunt today. We don't want things to get too competitive and you ruin your pretty dress."

"I can run just fine," I say, with a huff, practically daring someone to make a smart remark. I am completely incensed by seeing the others in jeans and sneakers, and it makes me feel like I'm wearing a costume instead of a dress.

They ought to have mailed an announcement ahead of time, but they didn't, which seems to have caused some confusion. And then my mother pulls out this dress, and I have this situation.

"It's a beautiful dress," Sister Diane assures, as if trying to temper my mood.

"Thank you," I say curtly, meaning *Get a good look at it because you'll never see it again.* At least I made it in time for the hunt with my gallon ice cream bucket with its metal handle, instead of one of those flimsy store-bought baskets I begin spotting others carrying.

Just about then, **Pastor Darrell** comes walking out of the parsonage with a handful of plastic grocery bags for those who forgot altogether. Even mad, I can't stop myself from grinning as he passes them around. The thin bags are too hard to open for depositing eggs during the fray. They tear easily and can't hold much weight.

I'm ten years old and I know that.

"Is everyone here now?" I ask loudly, meaning *Let's get this done so I can go change clothes and eat some candy.* I am at my own church, the Church of God, so I can be a bit more headstrong. My two best friends and I typically hit the egg hunts at the other three churches as well: the Baptist Church, the United Pentecostal Church, and another Church of God, just a few miles up the road.

Fellowship is stressed in the Word, after all.

This year, some of the egg hunts have overlapped, so we've had to divide and conquer. However, when the timing works out, the three of us together will hit all four churches to attend Vacation Bible Schools in the summer and various festivals, hay rides, and bonfires in the fall. We have perfected our marshmallow roasting routine (it starts by bringing our own wire-frame hangers). We enjoy a nice weenie roast too, especially if the church has a good budget for the event and springs for all-beef.

Sharp is like other small, Southern communities. The members of the different denominations generally know and like each other (at least publicly), even while quietly believing their own doctrine is superior. I'm not being ugly. The differences are as subtle as the length of a sleeve or whether a family's television is in the living room out in the open and all. That's how trivial the differences are to me. The height of my baby toenail is just about the height of my concern with it. And still, each church does support the others' events throughout the year.

In fact, my friends and I are at the four churches so much that I've come up with a single-word nickname for each one. Some of the staunch, long-standing saints might disapprove of this, seeing it as sacrilege.

I'm ten years old and I know that.

There's no use in pretending they'd be OK with it. But it is just that—a nickname. Pure and true.

Sharp Baptist Church I call "Lake" because it's across from CLECO Lake. Then there's Sharp United Pentecostal Church, which I've dubbed "Bricks" for the awkward red-brick add-on up front. My own church, Sharp Church of God, I've named "Pancakes" thanks to the pancake breakfast held the first Saturday of every month, and Highway 1 Church of God I call "Class," which is actually short for "high-class." It's the only church in the area that appears to have had some architectural thought put into its design. The Sunday School rooms are built around an open-air garden atrium. It just feels fancy.

I'd never pick favorites, but each church has its charms. Lake does a great Vacation Bible School. Their crafts are especially well-thought, usually ceramics we spend all week painting, culminating in the last night where we add the gilded rub to the edges and put them on display. Their graduation processional of VBS students in elaborate costumes based on the year's theme is impressive, too. My favorite so far has been "Kookaburra: Adventures in God's Glory," the Australian-based theme where we dressed as exotic animals from the outback. I was a proud kangaroo.

It probably goes without saying, but Bricks has the best music, hands down.

There's no other church music for me than something with a good beat and a strong alto voice. Old, chorded Pentecostal hymns like "One Less Stone (One More Voice to Praise Him)" or "I'll Have a New Body (Praise the Lord, I'll Have a New Life)" can really get your foot tapping. Bricks knows how to bring people in with a little singing from the diaphragm. The emphasis is typically on volume over vocal quality, but it's genuine. Or so it seems to me.

Class has a great gymnasium, and we use it often. With all the events held there, it feels like the heart of our community. It's the only gym around, actually, and anyone is allowed to book it by paying a small deposit and cleanup fee—except from mid-September to the end of October when they're setting up and operating their haunted house, *meaning their "Judgement House."* They put a lot of time and effort into it each year. It's an efficient way to lead people to the Lord while collecting five dollars a pop without passing a plate.

And finally, my church, the Sharp Church of God . . . well, that one should be self-explanatory. Who doesn't like pancakes?

Maybe these nicknames are too simple. Maybe they're even unfair as they don't capture the total picture. I like to strip a thing down to its fundamentals, find its essence. It's how I make sense of things, and I may take it too far.

In my mind, if you know something well enough to nickname it, you know it through and through.

Just like the eggs from the Easter egg hunt, some things are real, some are plastic. People, too.

And some people are weird. The people I know are.

My two best friends are Lah and Tut—LaDonna and Thomas, really. Lah lives next door, and Tut lives down the lane that curls behind her house. We're the same age and more like siblings than neighbors. You probably understand what that's like. **We know a lot of obscure things about each other.**

For instance, Lah has a floppy toe. No bones at all in the fourth toe on her right foot. She fusses constantly about how it folds up under her foot inside her shoe when she walks. I often see her taping it straight, even though she hates the gumminess of the tape and the loss of circulation if she wraps it too tightly.

And I could embarrass Tut any day of the week with the things I know about him—things you don't openly share with others for fear of getting *the look*. My earliest childhood memory of Tut is of him crying out. One Saturday morning at Pancakes, he bit into something (I assume a pancake) and out came a tooth. His mom helped him spit out the tooth and the bite of food into her hand. Then, after he'd rinsed his mouth with saltwater, she offered him the bite back. She'd been holding it. That's the look I mean. The look you're probably wearing now.

Everyone in my family has a nickname too. My older brother, Mason, goes by Big (only because he is the big brother of our three families as Lah and Tut have no siblings—*he's not actually big*). My name, Melissa, gets shortened to Missy, although Dad mostly calls me Little or sometimes just Lit.

Dad's nickname is Raym, short for Raymond. Lah started calling him this, and it stuck. She and Raym are two peas in a pod, both offbeat and over-the-top. Get them excited, and they'll jump up, shuffling and flapping their arms, with their heads tilted back, howling "YEEEWWWPEEE!" in exaggerated triumph.

It's their happy dance. Tut and I might roll our eyes, but we enjoy watching it. They're both ate up.

Lastly, there's my mother, Bingo. For years, she has sold Tupperware through the home party format and is known for her raucous games of Tupperware Bingo—which can get out of hand. You wouldn't believe how wild a group of church ladies can get over a free set of multi-colored Servalier bowls. It's fun to direct some good-natured raillery toward Bingo about Tupperware. She's consumed with it.

Visitors often stop by to peek inside our pantry at the solid wall of perfectly aligned canisters, complete with custom labels. Bingo is modest though, never letting on that it isn't just the pantry. Our closets are also outfitted with labeled Tupperware containers. I won't lie to you. She even has her panties separated inside her bureau drawers in Tupperware Square Rounds. Like the Servalier bowls, these come in a multi-color set, so it works well to assign a color to each day of the week.

Tut turns beet red anytime I bring up Bingo's panties, as he should I suppose.

Lah, Tut, and I spend the Saturday afternoon after the different egg hunts sprawled out on my front porch. Tut swings lazily, nibbling a chocolate-covered marshmallow egg, struggling to peel away the sticky foil in the afternoon heat. Lah and I sit in rocking chairs beneath the ceiling fan. She is organizing the candy to divide it according to our personal tastes, which, of course, she knows without asking. (I can't handle a Mr.

Goodbar or a Kit Kat. In fact, all of the chocolate goes to Tut. Lah prefers jelly beans, SweeTARTS, or Skittles, anything with a fruity flavor, and I have dibs on any miniature Charleston Chews, peanut butter bars, or Bit-O-Honeys.)

As we munch on candy, we can't help but laugh about Tut's luck. He spent the morning at Bricks to find that this year was a "Skip the Candy" hunt, and the plastic eggs were filled with slips of paper saying things like "Stay up an extra 30 minutes past bedtime," "Lunch date with mom," and "Choose a dessert."

The "great egg-tastrophe" I start calling it, laughing and irritating Tut, who's already fuming about this year's reduced candy haul. Somewhere in the distance, a dog barks, punctuating the air with its enthusiasm.

I rock back and forth in long, deliberate sweeps with my hands clasped over my stomach, scooping my head forward to gain momentum as I think.

"The hopocalypse!" I blurt out, grinning like I've struck gold. "That bunny didn't hop, did it?"

I start to add a bit of swagger to my head movements, and I can't erase the smirk on my face.

Lah's laughing so hard she's nearly choking on her Skittles, and I can see Tut's about to blow. He'd been taunting me earlier about the frilly dress I had to wear, though, so I'm not about to let up.

"Bad bunny," I mutter as I rock back and forth. "Bad, bad bunny." And then another hits me.

"The eggsplosion!" I shriek.

26

Tut throws his hands into the air, dropping them back into his lap and looking at me, exasperated.

"One day, Missy, that mouth of yours is gonna land you in trouble. You don't have to give everything a name!" he snorts, meaning *You're a smart-aleck.*

But Lah and I know that, even if we make him angry enough to get us down in a chokehold, we can always shift the situation in our favor. Especially Lah, because she's skilled at pulling emotion out of nowhere and puckering up like she's about to cry.

I wave away Tut's outburst, knowing he'll be over it by tomorrow's Easter Sunrise Service.

Just a few weeks later, Lah, Tut, and I are dragged by our parents to attend the high school's graduation. Pancakes is the smallest of the four churches, so when we have a graduate, we're expected to show support.

Graduations are always dreadful. Name after name called, with no one heeding the request to save applause until the end so the entire class can be honored at one time. This year, the high school is being renovated, so we're crammed into the gym at Class, where the acoustics are awful. With the size of the crowd, it's unbearable.

I am already miserable when I realize that, to top things off, the keynote speaker is a state representative from Baton Rouge. A *Democrat.*

There's nothing worse than listening to the rote address of a politician.

I smile during his speech as if he is impressing me, but I am so bored that I start studying the hanging steel trusses with their geometric shapes and the exposed air ducts that periodically force air out and make it especially difficult to hear, silver cylinders running long lengths to reach everyone. I tell myself that maybe the three of us can pitch in to stack the chairs afterwards, and there will be time to get a volleyball game in still. I can nag one of the older members of our youth group to drive us home.

The last graduate's name is finally called, the mortarboard caps are thrown into the air, and I beeline it to grab Tut and Lah to help with my plan.

With the air vents blowing full blast and parents and grandparents talking excitedly, the noise swells to a near-deafening hum. No one even notices as we start scraping the metal chairs loudly across the floor, stacking them, sometimes even rudely moving guests' belongings, as if we're rushing people out of there.

I decide to grab the few chairs that had been facing the audience, placed in front of pipe and drape to create a makeshift stage, and, in the gap between two of the flimsy cloth panels, I see Principal Jones and the representative, shaking hands and talking.

I take a chair to the cart we are stacking them on and come back for another. The buzz of chatter around me is heavy with pride and expectation.

"So, any of these kids going places?" the representative asks, having to speak loudly. "What's the expectation here—community college? Maybe a trade school?"

Principal Jones shrugs, glancing over his shoulder as if sharing a secret. "Honestly, most of them won't even leave town. Some will work nearby; the lucky ones might get a job at the electric plant. College isn't really on the table at all."

I had just picked up another chair but now stop short, holding it with its legs outward like the raised quills of a prickly porcupine. The metal feels cold in my grasp, a stark contrast to the warmth of the night's celebratory atmosphere. My heart races as I absorb their condescending words.

"Ah, I see," the representative replies, polite but with a hint of pity in his tone. He tilts his head to the side, raising his eyebrows. "Well, it's good they've got . . . options."

"Exactly," Principal Jones agrees, as if they're discussing an inevitable truth. "These are good kids, but we have to be realistic. They're not cut out for more."

I stiffen at that, the chair still in my hands, as the representative looks up and catches sight of me frozen there between the drapes.

He walks over with an outstretched hand. It's obvious he knows that I've heard what was just said, but he thinks his big smile can cover it.

"Thank you for helping with the cleanup," he says, and I put the chair down to shake his hand.

"This is Missy," Principal Jones says in a singsong voice, coming to introduce me with a flourish. "She's one of our brightest."

And then I guess I have what's called an epiphany—because I've had one before—just once when I saw the hope lined up in Dub Quincy's cemetery crosses. As I'm standing there, I'm thinking these two are labeling a girl who is now staring back at them angry, powerful. I am full of thoughts, willful thoughts, or at least a seething motivation. I can almost feel their assumptions pressing against me, a tangible force in the air, as if they've draped a heavy quilt of expectation over my small frame.

Nothing's wrong with staying close to home, of course, but the blatant dismissal enrages me, makes me strip them down and nickname them what they are. Phonies. I'm thinking, *Don't they know that it's most often the ordinary who do extraordinary things?* Just look at Jesus, the carpenter, after all.

These two men standing in the gym at Class underestimate me.

I'm ten years old and I know that.

"Happy to help," I say meaning *I'll show you one day. I will.*

Has any one supposed it lucky to be born?
I hasten to inform him or her it is just as lucky to
   die, and I know it.

—Walt Whitman, from *Song of Myself*

FOUR

Little Puppies in Heaven

(1982)

It all happened the summer when Lah and I were eleven. Tut had gone to Little Rock to spend June and July with his grandparents at their timeshare condo, so it was just the two of us—except for when my brother Big hung around.

Looking back, we should've known something was coming. Without Tut, things just seemed off-kilter, and we were running out of things to do. The long days stretched on, each one blending into the next. So when Raym and Bingo decided at the last minute that we should all pile into the motorhome and head out to the Central Louisiana Bluegrass Festival in Deville, we shrugged our shoulders and got in. Raym's friend, Donnell, was a well-known fiddler and was playing for the weekend in one of the headlining family bands.

Raym loved music festivals because of the chance to show off how he could play most stringed instruments by ear. He was best on the banjo or maybe the mandolin, but he also played the piano, all types of acoustic guitar and even the upright bass (known more commonly around here as the bull fiddle).

I have to confess. Even though it's not my type of music, I do kind of favor the bull fiddle.

A couple years back, Raym talked the rest of our family into participating in a Fifth Sunday Singsparation at the church, a sort of "come one, come all" amateur talent show.

We dressed in jeans, boots, and blue-checkered shirts that Bingo had made just for the performance, matching down to the last detail. Big was 13 and I was nine, and Raym had taught us "Just Over in the Glory Land," so we surprised everyone and performed together as a family band—Raym on banjo, Big on guitar, and *me on the bull fiddle*!

Bingo stood off to the side and bumped the tambourine against her leg.

I don't exactly know how we pulled it off. We only knew the one song, and I'm sure we were a sight. I was a little thing and had to just get up there and stand at the top of the center aisle in front of the altar table, smiling, until one of the deacons could bring me the bull fiddle. I think they first thought I was up there to sing.

I saw some in the congregation of the Sharp Church of God grinning a little too big and kind of covering their mouths when Brother Martin stood the fiddle in front of me; he paused a minute with his hands spread wide as if he might need to catch it. When he finally sat down, the audience wasn't sure how to react or what was to come. (I later learned that Tut and Lah were on the floor holding their stomachs.)

But our family band brought the house down, especially when we repeated the last refrain:

Just oh . . . (doom doom) . . . ver in the gloryland;
There with . . . (doom doom) . . .
the mighty host I'll stand (rest)
Just over in the gloryland (doom doom doom doom)

We ended the song to a standing ovation.

Some were probably worried that I'd tip over with the heavy bull fiddle, but I'd kept a bulldog grip on the neck, plucking the beat just like Raym taught me.

It was a moment, for sure. So when we loaded up to go to the festival, this all came flooding right back, and I was glad Raym was bringing the fiddle.

Nights in the motorhome were something.

Lah and I were the smallest, so we'd bunk above the captain's chairs. The crawlspace was room enough, but Lah had a bizarre phobia about sleeping on colored bedding. The dark brown, velvety mattress was too much, especially in a confined space. She avoided having a panic attack by sleeping with her arms stretched over her head and her palms pressed to the camper wall. Periodically, she'd have to lick her palms and reposition. Licking her palms and sticking them flat grounded her, made her feel alright.

And then there was Bingo, who always had to "tee." Always. For those in earshot, it sure seemed like she could have saved it up and at least gone *tinkle tinkle* instead of the furtive *tink* she woke us up for, stumbling over Raym's guitar and banjo cases and smacking down the toilet lid each time. At the very least, she could've held off on *the flush* and *the blow*. I'm not sure what it was about "teeing" that made her habitually have to blow her nose, but *the flush* and *the blow* were both invariable parts of her routine.

And finally, Bingo didn't go anywhere without Boo Boo, our family's old mean Siamese (his real name was Beauregard).

Boo Boo had a vicious temper, delicate eating habits, and, routinely, a urinary tract infection. It took a long time to learn Boo Boo's ways, and just when you thought you knew what to expect from him, he'd take the hide off the back of your hand for accidentally touching his ears or for trying to slide his food bowl to him incorrectly. His bowl had to be pushed over to him sideways-like with only a finger. It had to look like you were trying to sneak it to him. No eye contact could be made. It was also important to hang around, as when Boo Boo finished 27 morsels of his special sensitive-stomach cat food, someone had to be ready to turn on the kitchen faucet so he could lap his weight in water.

Big, Lah, and I were used to Boo Boo, but it didn't make it any easier to travel with him in the motorhome. There was a yellow towel carefully covering one end of the RV's couch. It was Boo Boo's daytime spot where he had a great window view. At night, when the couch opened up to become Raym and Bingo's bed, Boo Boo relocated to the small back bedroom where Big slept. Though Big had the nicest bed, there wasn't much of it left once the mandolin, banjo, acoustic guitar, and bull fiddle—all in their oversized cases—were stacked on it, and he didn't get any sleep for fear of rolling over and having his face spit-shined and razored.

Boo Boo, who was well-known by festival goers, had become as much of an enduring legend as the "Foggy Mountain Breakdown" or "Orange Blossom Special." He was respected for the way he sat on that yellow towel, watching from his perch.

The center of the festival was a massive flea market housed in and around the Thomas Jason Lingo Community Center, so, the next morning, while Raym and Bingo set chairs out under the canopy, unpacked the instruments, and got settled, Lah and I headed there to explore. We were looking forward to a fun day. There's nothing better than eating a fresh funnel cake covered in powdered sugar outdoors on a crisp, summer morning.

Plus, Raym's sister, my crazy Aunt Mackie, was planning to drive up for the afternoon concert. She'd gone to high school with Donnell, so she was excited about seeing him play too. He'd hit the big time.

Like Raym, Mackie was a dynamo who loved to jump right into a jam session. Except it was with her accordion, and usually with a mutter about how her titty hurt from squeezing it between the bellows. She also kept a tambourine in the trunk of her car, alongside her accordion, "just in case."

Lah and I had not seen Mackie in action at a festival before, but we never wanted to miss a minute of her wherever she was. In fact, Raym had joked earlier that morning that he'd have to go retrieve her car later as she never had the patience to find their camping spot. She'd park anywhere and walk until she found him or until she could join a group huddled under a tree playing music.

She was something.

I shouldn't tell this, but one time she was sitting by me in church, and I guess she was bored with the sermon because she took my weekly bulletin and doodled all over it with the ballpoint reserved on the pew back for use with the tithing envelopes. During the offering and a special duet sung by Sister Clovis Allen and Sister Sarah Knight, I leaned over and complimented her work, whispering that she could draw a lovely fleur-de-lis.

Mackie started giggling. It was a gentle shoulder shimmy at first, with one hand covering her mouth, but then she really struggled not to make a scene she got to laughing so hard. I was worried Sister Clovis and Sister Sarah were going to think we were laughing at their rendition of "Consider the Lilies," which was off-time, but still quite nice, when, with me cutting eyes at her to stop, she rasped, "It's not a fleur-de-lis. *It's a peter*!"

Quickly drawing a few more all over the page before replacing the pen and grasping the offering plate to pass it down the row, she leaned over and whispered again, "I've always liked drawing little peters," just like she was talking about drawing a daisy!

I couldn't believe a grown-up could be so crazy. I loved her for that. Still do.

Anyway, it was near noon when Lah and I started back toward our camp, passing rows and rows of all sizes of RVs and huddles of people at picnic tables. We were tired of walking through the crowded booths of homemade jewelry, embroidered pet collars, and other crafts, and near sick from eating deep-fried Twinkies on top of our funnel cakes. We were talking about how Bingo would be frustrated that we'd spoiled the lunch she'd packed in her special Tupperware divided plates that were not available for public sale, when we heard a siren in the distance.

Neither of us gave the sound a second thought at first; ambulances and fire trucks were easy entertainment for kids at a festival. We knew that we were camped on the fifth row on the left side just past the cinderblock building housing the communal restrooms and showers.

But as we kept walking, we saw the ambulance . . . saw it in motion with a red utility truck parting people and leading it through the maze as quickly as it could under the circumstances . . . saw it turn onto the makeshift grass road of *the fifth row.*

We started to run.

Hearts pounding, we followed the ambulance and stopped short when, just ahead of us, we were suddenly blocked from seeing by both the ambulance and a crowd outside our RV.

I pushed through, panicking, and found Raym kneeling over a man lying on the ground.

"Donnell . . ." Raym was pleading. "Donnell . . . let me try . . ." Raym was using his fingers to try to get a man to open his mouth.

Donnell was grasping his throat, making a sound that would've been a scream if he'd been able to get it out; he seemed desperate and fearful. He rolled to the side and tried to spit; it was like he was trying to move his tongue out of the way and keep his mouth open to bring something up but, perhaps in shock, at the same time wanted to hold it all in. He pressed both palms against his chest as if it would help with his effort.

Two paramedics came rushing in with heavy bags. A third trailed behind, struggling to push a wheeled bed on the uneven grass. I barely breathed as they assessed the situation, their faces unreadable. Even as Raym pleaded with his friend, they were checking vital signs.

Raym persisted with his attempts to help, but Donnell was losing consciousness and his jaws were locked with his lips parted slightly. I remember thinking that he looked like a man stuck in the 1950s, with his slick dark hair, boots, jeans, and plaid western shirt.

The paramedics started CPR, and the crowd was beginning to back away a few steps, scared of looking too closely, when, after a few compressions, Donnell startled everyone by suddenly opening his eyes.

He jerked to a seated position, looking around wildly.

No one moved or spoke as Donnell surveyed the crowd, seemingly taking a moment to look at each one and make a connection. His gaze lingered on Raym, a flicker of recognition breaking through the haze of confusion.

"All . . . of life . . . is a song . . ." he sputtered.

He appeared to have more to say, a great orator poised to speak momentous words. But then, he grabbed Raym's arm and fell back, his head to the side, a tiny splatter of blood seeping out to dot his chin.

Though the paramedics jumped into gear with more chest compressions, they were unable to revive him.

People were shaking their heads and looking down, the way you do when trying to show sympathy but don't know what to say. Some were whispering quietly in little groups, explaining to others what had happened. A dense stillness settled over the crowd, thick with disbelief, as if the very fabric of the day shifted.

Lah had found a lawn chair and was taking off her right shoe to straighten up her floppy toe from all the running. That toe was the very thing that endeared her to Mackie, who had undergone minor surgery to shorten her own second toe, being embarrassed by how it stuck out too far. Until the surgery, she wouldn't wear sandals, and Lah could so readily relate.

Mackie saw Lah sitting there with her shoe off and went to rub her hand up and down her back.

"I can't believe this is happening," Lah murmured, glancing back at the commotion.

And then there was Raym. He sat down hard on the RV's steps and dropped his head into his hands, sobbing.

Boo Boo was in the window looking out.

It was a freak accident, a one-in-a-million circumstance that could not be predicted or foreseen. Listening to those standing around, we learned that Donnell had choked to death on the lever tab from a can of Yoo-hoo. The "pull tab" had been out of circulation on aluminum soda cans for years, but as Donnell had always done with no repercussions, he had rocked the levered tab back and forth until it came off and then dropped it down into the can. The habit had become fatal.

Of course, we left the festival that day.

Even Boo Boo seemed upset about the incident. When we got home, he went and laid in his litter box for days. I'm not sure if he had actually witnessed death from the window or if he simply sensed how we all felt, but in a strange way his sadness was appreciated and we became defensive of him, and motherly. Though we tried to take special care of him, Boo Boo gradually became more and more lethargic.

A few weeks later, we found him one morning and at first thought he was asleep; he was curled into a tight ball on the kitchen counter near the faucet. That cat was thirsty all his life.

Boo Boo was 18 years old when he died, something unheard of for a cat that could go outside in the country, where cars and coyotes could get him. He had been a special treasure to Bingo.

She carefully wrapped him in soft rags. Then, she put him in a Tupperware Cake Taker and sealed it herself, burping the lid so that his little coffin was airtight.

That afternoon, Raym gingerly buried the rounded dome among the daylilies outside the kitchen window. We had a little service, too. Bingo, Big, Lah, and I stood in a circle around the hole that had been dug. Lah came up with some words to say because Bingo was too choked up to speak.

Mackie was there and played her accordion. The mournful notes carried our sadness, the natural volume of the instrument catching the attention of passersby on the highway who honked their horns.

Burying Boo Boo seemed to be the last straw for Raym.

It felt to him that things he'd always known were temporal and somehow slipping because, *my goodness*, we even lost the cat.

None of us realized it at first, but Raym started going over to the cemetery every evening. There, he dragged a chair from the pavilion, placed it next to the single grave tucked between a pair of oak trees, and talked to his friend, Donnell.

Eventually, Mackie learned what Raym was doing and started joining him. While he sat lost in thought, she walked the cemetery, noting the names on the memorials and mentally connecting the generations to see if she could account for all of the families who had loved ones buried there. She walked and walked, coming back to Raym often to tell him about people Donnell should expect to see in heaven. By studying the names she saw, she learned a lot about the families in the community.

Mackie explained that the Fletchers had lost an infant at birth, that their old childhood neighbor, Ed Beebe, had a twin brother who had been killed in a head-on collision, that the Allens had lost a daughter who was a high school senior struggling with leukemia and trying to survive until graduation. She lived just two weeks past that mark.

The more Mackie talked about the people Donnell should look for in heaven, the more Raym began to feel a sense of communion, realizing that there was a story to every headstone. Gradually, he came to believe that he wasn't alone in the way he felt about Donnell. There were others whose deaths seemed even more senseless than choking to death while drinking a can of Yoo-hoo.

Raym began to leave his chair and walk the cemetery with Mackie, reading the names and loving words on the headstones aloud as if Donnell was walking with them. He explained to Donnell as best he could who each person was.

Sometimes, later at night, he called families to ask about their loved ones, saying he was trying to connect the names he saw to those in the community. He explained that he'd been spending a lot of time at the cemetery and that, well, he just wanted to know who was there.

In July 1982, Raym and a few others began to collect and formally document all of their research to piece together a history of the families represented in the cemetery. Bingo helped the Eastern Star ladies plan out a special quilt, with each family's name embroidered on a square. More and more people had begun to take interest in knowing their ancestry and relation to the cemetery.

Everyone he called was proud to talk about their own.

Raym's mood slowly lightened; it was an awakening of sorts. The more he learned about the departed, the more he wanted to understand what it was like "over there." He just wanted to know that those who left this earth early were not cheated, that they were, actually, rewarded more abundantly.

It was a simple thing really.

Because he had personally witnessed someone's life end, he wanted an understanding of what was next. He reasoned that if he knew that friends were sitting in rocking chairs on a front porch waiting on him to get there, then he could look forward to his own death, and perhaps live with a little more abandon.

Mackie constantly reassured Raym that heaven was pure, soft, and good—*so good, in fact, that there would be little puppies there*. And Raym believed it. His faith had never wavered. But there was still something pulling him toward a greater understanding of the "song" Donnell referred to. He had an idea . . .

Two weeks later, Raym abruptly stood up during the dinner on the grounds of the annual graveyard working, asking for everyone's attention. He announced that he was planning a congé at the cemetery the following Saturday at 2 p.m. He had been reading and learned that a congé was a final farewell. It was a ceremony to say goodbye without the formality and sadness of a funeral.

Raym expressed his hope that everyone would join him to celebrate the joy their loved ones had brought them, but he made it clear that he would be there regardless.

With that, he sat down and not much else was said that day. No one knew what to think about the whole thing, but people were interested in the idea.

The week passed in a flutter.

The groundskeepers were called to ensure the grass was perfectly groomed. Many put fresh flowers on their family's graves. Even the place markers, the ground-level stones that simply mark future gravesites, were brushed and cleaned so that the engraved names were clearly identifiable.

When Saturday came, Bingo and I headed to the cemetery a few minutes early with Big. She'd spent the last week working furiously to finish the community quilt, and she wanted us to help hang it as a centerpiece on the gate before others arrived.

But we were not ahead of anyone at all.

Following the narrow lane and rounding the last curve before the dense woods open into the sprawling grounds of Campbell Creek Cemetery, still nearly a quarter mile away, we were awestruck to encounter cars lining the road on both sides. We carefully continued on, and, seeing us, people slowly began getting out to stand awkwardly, not quite sure what to do, but determined to be there. It was as if the entire crowd was holding its breath, waiting for something none of us could define. They had arrived ahead of time, and now they waited for someone to lead them.

Out of respect, Big had already planned to open the cemetery gate for Raym—in case no one showed up. But faced with a crowd, he suddenly sensed his own part in the day and felt the weight of his role more deeply.

With just the slightest brake of the car, a hesitation only because of the surprise of seeing so many, Big boldly became sure of himself. He drove on to the gate, leaving the car running as he quickly helped Bingo and me pull the heavy quilt from its huge Tupperware box and drape it at the entrance. We made sure that all the names were clearly displayed, the embroidered letters bearing witness to the memories they honored.

Then, while Bingo and I found a place to wait for everyone walking up, Big swung the gate wide, secured it back, and quickly parked just inside the entrance.

Meanwhile, Raym had just lifted the door of his special garage where he always kept some sort of antique car and pulled out in his freshly washed and waxed Model A convertible. Colorful balloons popped into the air as soon as they were clear of the door—a huge bouquet of vibrant hues floated high, tethered by long, streaming white ribbons. Tin cans, tied with string, clattered and trailed from the back bumper, which was made from polished chrome and gleamed in the summer sun.

Mackie sat beside Raym with her accordion on her lap, smiling broadly as if she had a secret.

Lah was in the rumble seat with boxes of rose petals on either side.

And so it was that two months, almost to the day, after Donnell died, Raym purposefully drove through the narrow passage created by cars positioned in respectful formation on either side of the cemetery road, and the people parted and fell in line walking behind him.

When Raym reached Big just inside the gate, he paused and acknowledged him with a subtle nod of appreciation. Then, Raym allowed Mackie to step out and swing her accordion strap around her neck, the familiar weight giving her a sense of purpose.

In a move that would've been strange any other day, Big stood tall in formal military salute, his posture exuding a calm strength meant to give courage to the insecurely approaching families. With his chest puffed out, he held the salute a heartbeat longer, as if anchoring everyone in the surreal moment.

Mackie was wearing her Sunday best and had her hair in a thick high bun as she began to lead the march behind the car, singing out loudly the opening verse of "Everybody will be Happy Over There" in a cappella:

While all four churches of Sharp and several outside denominations were represented by those walking behind her (some families had even called in Catholic relatives from out of town), no one could deny a good Pentecostal hymn led by a sure, strong voice.

So when Mackie added her accordion for accompaniment as she launched into the chorus, the crowd unabashedly responded en masse with the well-known refrain:

It was easy then. With Mackie proudly leading, the united congregation suddenly had the confidence of those whose faith is sure and who know that inhibitions in this life are trivial and fleeting. Mackie continued marching around the cemetery grounds, moving from hymn to hymn and even to "When the Saints Go Marching In."

I'm sure she winced from squeezing her titty as she went.

The walkers that lagged in the back soon surged forward, feeling empowered, and joined the others to form an impressive and resounding procession behind Raym and the Model A. Lah stood, facing backwards, throwing rose petals from the rumble seat to form a delicate pink and red carpet for the feet of those on parade.

And the feeling of the day changed from tentative to jubilant. The participants held framed photographs, colorful handmade signs, flowers, and even teddy bears, and joyfully raised their relics up for others to see. One man wobbled through on the bicycle of his young son whom he had lost to bone cancer at age seven.

The person for whom each walked, at that moment, hovered so close.

Not a tear was shed.

It was hard to believe that Raym had a parade *at the cemetery* and that he genuinely *celebrated* there. With music. And singing. And laughter.

I couldn't believe how many people joined in, supporting his intent—even if they didn't understand the event itself. While Raym was certainly known for his eclectic ideas, this one topped them all.

Undeniably, the congé was life-changing for many in the community, awakening their memories of loved ones and replacing their sense of loss with renewed hope. It reopened a connection that was typically considered closed at the time of death. It spawned a new way of thinking for Lah and me, too. The odd experience left behind a mystical feeling, a calming presence, a new understanding of the softness of life.

It was hard to explain this to Tut.

"There's one thing I definitely believe about heaven now," I told him on a three-way call later that night. Lah had just finished bragging about her queen-like role in the lead car, flinging rose petals from the rumble seat. She was distracted and barely listening.

"There will be little puppies there, warm and soft," I continued, my voice dreamy with the memory of all that had transpired.

"*Puppies*, Missy?" Tut asked, incredulous, not sure he'd heard correctly.

"Yes," I asserted, but didn't explain further.

As my two best friends bantered on, I wasn't on the call at all. Closing my eyes, I was lost in reverie of nuzzling my face into soft, puppy ears—realizing, with a start, that it was Jesus.

Swiftly arose and spread around me the peace and
   knowledge that pass all the argument of the earth,
And I know that the hand of God is the promise
   of my own,
And I know that the spirit of God is the brother
   of my own,
And that all the men ever born are also my
   brothers . . .

—Walt Whitman, from *Song of Myself*

FIVE

So Great a Cloud of Witnesses

(1984-1989)

We were in the creek baptizing each other in Jesus' name when the sound cut through. I had just griped about how roughly Lah had dunked Tut, creating a tidal wave that made the grungy water overflow into my pink polka-dotted rubber roots.

"It's too fast," I said.

I knew, though, that Lah had little control over how gracefully she put Tut under. Being somewhat ample and compressed, Tut was lucky that Lah, 95 pounds soaking wet, could raise him into his new life at all. My brother, Big, was mowing a neighbor's yard to make some spending money that Saturday morning, so without him there, Lah depended on the bulbous toes of her boots to bumper Tut's head, help buoy him back up above the water's surface.

Tut managed not to drown, but he was grumpy.

We were 12 that summer, and, as usual, Lah had been laughing too hard to finish the preaching, so we just pretended the spirit had gotten ahold of us and started shouting—dancing around, flailing our arms in the air like we'd been doused in fire ants. Our familiarity with small, country churches had given us plenty to mimic, all leading up to the big baptism finale. The baptism part of our service was always last and often created an argument, mainly because no one wanted to be the newly redeemed sinner who got totally soaked.

It was a June morning, and the air was crisp and still. The only sounds were natural—the trickling of water through fallen branches that had been woven together by the current's flow, the chirping of birds with their high-pitched voices insisting "we need you, we need you," and the gurgling, airy slurp of rubber boots as they were lifted from heavy, wet sand.

So we stopped short when we heard it.

There was a heavy *clang* and a shoulder-to-ear lifting *screech* and then a loud *slam!* Cutting through our squealing and laughter was the out-of-place, unmistakable clash of metal on metal. Though unsure of the entirety of of the sound, the last part was an old pickup's tailgate being forcefully shut. I am from the South, and—without seeing, without a doubt—that was what it was.

Lah and I paused, sharing a brief, collective hush as we tried to identify the source.

"It's nothing," Tut said, seeing the two of us wide-eyed. He was sitting up in the shallow creek, sliding his hands down the length of his arms as if to squeegee out the water.

Lah and I had already started clambering toward the sound though, dragging our feet against the burden of the current. I got to the bank first, quickly finding the tree with exposed roots that we used for footholds, but in my hurry, I slipped. My wet boots felt especially clunky, and I wildly grabbed at vines as I scrambled up the embankment, breath heavy and heart racing.

When I finally hauled myself onto solid ground, I barely caught a glimpse of a thin man, dark hair falling across his forehead, rolling up the sleeves of a plaid shirt as he lunged behind the wheel.

The old green pickup jolted into gear, brake lights flaring red like a warning. He didn't hesitate, didn't even look my way. He just gunned it. The engine growled, spitting dust and loose gravel as he shot forward.

"Wait! Wait!" I shouted, my voice swallowed by the quickening thrum of tires on dirt. And then he was gone, leaving behind only the wisp of exhaust and the uneasy prickle of being watched.

My chest tightened. It felt as though he'd slipped away like a thief in the night, leaving only unease in his wake. He had to have seen me. Honestly, I had a shivery feeling then. Like you're going about your ordinary business in your usual way, only to suddenly catch a glint and realize it's the voyeuristic eyes of someone peeping at you.

It was creepy, really. By the time Lah was beside me on the bank, all she could do was look back and forth from me to the open space and the crude tracks in the high grass in front of us. Tut, always moving in his own time, finally came up behind us.

"Somethin' happen, Missy?" he asked.

We stood there quietly for a moment, unsure what to make of things. There were never any vehicles, other than ATVs, down by the creek. We didn't even know it was possible. What had he thrown into the bed of that truck? Tools? It was definitely something solid and metal. *And had he been watching us?*

I felt the cold air and realized how wet I was from that morning's baptism.

"Whatever he was doing—whoever it was—is gone," Lah eventually said.

Tut wasn't giving it a second thought, and that was seemingly the end of it for Lah, too.

I wanted to let it go, I really did, but I've never been the kind of person who could shrug things off. Once something lodged itself in my head, it gnawed at me, pulling me back to it over and over until I could make sense of it. And I've never been able to keep my life simple. Whenever something happens, I always have to know the exact reason for it. So I was all in, complicit. Ignoring it felt willfully negligent, like holding a book of instructions against my chest instead of opening it for its wisdom.

With my hands on my hips, I was still standing there, pensive, looking in the direction of the truck.

"Fool," Tut snarked, shaking his head at me.

But even though he blew it off, I knew we all felt strange about it. It was quite a trek through the woods behind our houses to the creek.

In our close-knit community, there was no one, even if he had managed to drive a truck there, who would act so mysteriously as to hightail it upon us seeing him. Most people would stop and visit, or they'd laugh and "play church" with us. There was definitely more to it.

Our clothes dripping with water, we started walking toward home.

Going forward, Tut would frequently tease me about the story I'd made up about a man in an old pickup when we'd *literally never*, he'd stress, seen a vehicle anywhere near the creek in our whole lives. Sometimes, he took his jokes too far, laughing and wiggling his fingers in my face the way people do when they tell ghost stories and want to scare those listening.

"Ooooh. Maybe someone was trying to find a place to bury a dead body," he'd taunt.

It became an uncomfortable ribbing between us, a festering sore spot. He told the story often, repeating it in various settings with new embellishments to embarrass me. He liked to embarrass me.

"Missy even said the man had dark, wavy hair, sort of like Jesus," he would tell everyone.

"So . . . just because *you* didn't see him, *you* don't believe it even happened, Thomas?" I would hiss.

I always called him by his real name when I was mad at him. Every time he put on that smirk, exaggerating the details, it made my throat burn, like I was holding back words that would scorch me if I let them out.

Lah often had to break us up or we'd fight about it.

A couple years later, the three of us rallied Raym to spend his Labor Day weekend helping us build a fort on a narrow ridge on the other side of the creek bank. It was near the old, decaying, leaning tree with exposed roots—the trusted spot we often used to climb out—and provided a great vantage point in both directions to see the creek's picturesque winding deep into the woods.

Plus, in this specific spot, we'd eventually discovered since *the incident* that there actually was enough of a beaten path to drive supplies down in a truck. Big slowly drove Raym's truck while we walked ahead ensuring there were no obstacles that would cause any problems. He was done after that and left the project to us.

Tut had been the most passionate about the idea of building the fort, and his enthusiasm was contagious. In the weeks before, he and Raym made a rough sketch, penciling and erasing many times before going to gather the supplies, mostly leftover scraps collected from various neighbors.

When we began construction, he was organized and stuck to his plan. He worked harder than any of us as he dragged three old railroad ties one by one out of the truck bed to be the main supports. They were black and still sticky with creosote, and it was difficult to drag them across the shallow creek to the other side. Between the ties, he planned to brace fence posts to create a V-shaped space with its opening toward the water. He'd also gotten two old, white king-sized sheets from Bingo to hang for the sides.

I remember the up and down motion as the posthole digger cut into the ground. It was violent and the dirt made a sort-of crunching sound as it was broken and lifted away. The slow process was hard work.

And then, when the hole for the first tie was roughly only 18-inches deep, the blades of the digger landed with a *chink!* and seemed to bounce back up.

We all stopped what we were doing at the sound.

It was obvious that the impact stung Raym's hands. After opening and closing his fingers into fists for a minute and rubbing the insides of his palms, he grimaced and tried again, hitting the same hard obstruction.

Raym shrugged and stopped only long enough to rub his palms once again before deciding to move back a few feet to start a new hole.

"Must be some settled rock there," he said, not giving it a second thought. We were relieved when we began to see the dirt heaped high beside that new hole.

The railroad ties, our cornerstones, were the longest part of the day.

Lah held a tie steady in the center of each hole, and we added small stones in an even circle to help brace the tie while Tut poured the cement he'd mixed in a five-gallon bucket. After the footings hardened, adding the fence posts went quickly.

We stayed into the evening, pleaching branches we'd pulled from the woods to create a thatch roof. We crudely attached grommets along the top edges of the sheets and used zip ties to hang them. I noticed that Raym's face was scratched up as, not knowing any better, some of the branches we'd chosen were laden with briers and thorns. He never said anything as we carelessly slung them around, trying to get them positioned to be the crown jewel atop our sanctuary. Being the tallest, we had inadvertently lashed him in the face in our attempts to get the branches up high enough for the makeshift roof.

I couldn't believe all Dad did for us that day. He worked in silence, never asking for anything in return, only smiling when he saw our excitement. His patience seemed endless, like the day itself.

When we were finally finished and surveyed our work, we noticed a pre-drilled hole in the center railroad tie. Instead of being exactly in the middle, from side to side, the hole was a bit over to the right. This left me curious. The hole's smooth edge made it clear it had served a purpose. Now buried halfway in the ground, it formed a small cavern, like a hidden well, that sent my imagination spinning.

I liked the mystical nature this hole added to our fort. I envisioned tucking folded notes into the cavern as part of a secret ritual. I could easily dream up reasons why we had discovered it half-buried the way we did. I got excited about the idea of explaining our fort to others then, and that we planned for the hidden hollow to be in the center tie all along.

It was a fine fort, indeed; the handiwork was impressive by any standard.

We spent a lot of time there the rest of that year. And the next few years. Often, we would sit on the ground and each lean back against one of the three supports with our legs pointing toward the center—our feet practically touching—forming a three-spoked wheel. The fort felt like it was ours alone, a place where the rest of the world couldn't reach us.

We would talk long into the night, occasionally building the tiniest of campfires, never getting scared even in the pitch blackness. We knew the area so well and were confident we could walk home in minutes.

That fort with its three ties was the perfect representation of how we grew up—three, but one.

We talked about everything there, with the subjects gradually maturing. We complained about our science teacher, Ms. Dutton. Until January 28, 1986.

That day, Ms. Dutton rolled in a TV on a cart for our class, and we were all watching and waiting with expectancy—only to witness every detail of the Space Shuttle Challenger exploding in mid-air just 73 seconds after liftoff. In classrooms throughout the school, students and teachers alike stayed where they were and watched for the next few hours, ignoring the bells that signaled class changes. Ms. Dutton was pretty broken up about the tragic end for fellow-teacher Christa McAuliffe; the way she acted that day softened how we thought about her. That tragedy seemed to shift something in all of us, lingering in the quiet pauses in our conversations.

We talked about feeling limited living in such a small community, too protected, too known. It was hard to think about leaving, but it was harder to think about staying. We wanted to live somewhere that was big enough to allow the freedom to mess up without everyone knowing, though we had no idea what "messing up" entailed.

We talked about who we'd like to date and who we'd been warned not to. There were few options, and the conversation circled back around to being too protected and too known. These were our young teenage years, so, within the conversations, you can imagine the sarcasm, the giggling, the teasing about who had boobs (including Tut). There was the shared anxiety of the practice portion of Driver's Ed, with old Coach Poe sitting to the right pumping the brake in the specially-made student car, adding to our stress about crashing.

And periodically, just every once in a while, we talked about the biggest things. Like what we believed, what we knew for sure.

That fort, maybe because it was secluded, often made me think of a Sunday School lesson about when young David hid from Saul deep in a cave in the wilderness. Perhaps because of the tiny well in the center tie, I loved the idea of a hiding place.

The same way David found refuge in the cave, the fort gave us a sense of security. But I couldn't ignore how it also mirrored the way we felt about Sharp itself—a place that sheltered us but could also close us off from the wider world. The very thing that protected us was also the thing that kept us tethered. It was a double-edged sword, a cleft in the rock that was both a sanctuary and a trap.

Later in the Bible story, Saul also enters a cave, unaware that David is so close that he is able to cut off a piece of his robe. Surely Saul felt chills when he later realized how near David had been all along.

And the kindness of David! That always got me. His kindness transformed the secret hiding place into something divine, a cleft in the rock where grace dwelled. That hidden nearness, the sense of being watched over, lingered like a silent comfort, both in the Bible story and in our own lives.

The fort was our hangout, the place to which we always returned, especially during our high school years. Four years older than us, Big had gone on to college and never knew the fort in the same way as the three of us.

I still thought sporadically about the *incident*, that day when the truck and man had come and gone. Even years later, there was the frustration of trying to explain something mysterious without losing the conviction of its legitimacy. Plus, such close friends shouldn't have to convince each other of anything.

Still, on this, Tut would never budge.

In 1989, at our high school graduation, the keynote speaker was the pastor from Sharp Baptist Church, Brother James Beebe. His initial comments were typical and predictable. He talked about the importance of making smart decisions and having solid foundations in life, about choosing the right person to marry, and about seriously considering staying in our community.

He hoped that we'd all continue on to college and that we'd return again to build a life there.

With his dark hair slicked back just enough that it shined slightly (and a little too long for most folks to trust him as a preacher), I decided he had the look of that stereotypical image of Jesus used for flannel board cutouts for Vacation Bible Schools and modeled after in passion plays. Maybe I thought lots of people looked like Jesus, who knows, but there was definitely a comfortable familiarity about him.

I mentally deemed him Graduation Jesus.

He drew us in with his words. A mood of veneration seemed to fall that made the nickname appropriate.

We all began to listen intently to this voice that was so kind, so understanding. Up and down the rows, the cardboard funeral fans had stopped waving. Everyone was leaning forward as if to block out distractions to the right or left.

Tut, sitting one row ahead of me since we were in alphabetical order for the processional, was right in my line of sight. Maybe it was just a sentimental moment since the comments had us looking back wistfully over our youth, but Graduation Jesus had us hanging on his every word. I could tell that even Tut was entranced like there was a voice speaking directly into his ear.

"This is a special day," Jesus said. "I've seen a lot of you grow up, playing in Campbell Creek, running a bit wild, just like I did."

He laughed, tapped two fingers to his eyes, then pointed them toward all of us, playfully signaling that he'd been keeping an eye on us.

"Some of you have been baptized a few more times than necessary," he quipped with a kind smile.

Tut spun around and cut eyes at Lah and me to indicate we'd been busted.

It was a humorous, light-hearted moment that simply acknowledged the antics of kids, but slowly something startling began to unravel and run right down to my core as I realized *he'd seen us.*

Jesus continued his comments with everyone engaged and laughing. His eyes misted over. He thought for a long moment, studying the crowd, seemingly changing what he was going to say on a whim, or maybe just feeling the connection with the audience.

"Did you know that there are 722 references to water in the Bible?" he asked.

He thought for another moment, seemed to look inward, unsure of how much to reveal.

"Did you know that our creek narrows and widens at various points and, in some places, may appear as though it has dried up, but it actually winds through Sharp and all the way out to the cemetery? It's easy to overlook it, but it's always been there, shaping the land and the lives around it."

He took a quick drink from a bottle of water tucked beneath the podium before he continued.

"I mention the creek because graduation is a time of marking new beginnings while reflecting on where we've come from. Consider all the saints from our community who rest in Campbell Creek Cemetery, and that water flowing back out from there to where kids play. Well . . . it may sound crazy, but I've always believed that creek is sacred, almost like a stream from heaven. Those banks hold memories—the kind we bury sometimes, not to forget, but to honor."

He looked at his watch.

"I've gone on too long. I didn't mean to be overly sentimental, but I do think we are all connected in a way that transcends this life and reaches into forever."

And then Jesus sat down. His words were dramatic and poetic, but sincere.

I think we all realized that we weren't ourselves sitting there in the hard, metal folding chairs lined neatly in the high school gymnasium. We were our mothers and fathers, our grandparents, anyone who'd gone before, anyone who'd played in that same creek. It was a reminder of how paths are intertwined, and that the story is still unfolding. It made me feel as though we were being led along a particular road in turn, and though we'd made certain stops—just like the Roman Road to Salvation with its specific markers of gold, black, red, white, and green—we weren't at our destination yet. Perhaps there were colors yet to know.

A graduation party followed. Our three families, living so close, knowing each other so well, celebrated together. Along with the gifts and congratulations, our parents teased us about the many predicaments we'd gotten into over the years, and, naturally, mentioned the keynote speaker's humorous remarks about our version of baptisms in the creek.

In their eyes, we would forever be their children, which, I'm sure, is how all parents want it to be.

Raym reminded us of the fort he'd helped us build five years before.

"It's pretty run down now, but it was sure special," he said. Raym's voice trailed off, and we all became nostalgic, lost in thought.

Memories of laughter and late-night conversations flooded back, intertwining with the bittersweet taste of growing up. In that moment, we weren't just friends; we were a tapestry of shared experiences, each thread woven tightly into the others.

And then suddenly Tut knew.

Running outside, he searched a moment and grabbed a shovel from the shed.

He didn't wait for us.

Lah and I tried to catch up, but he ran so fast. Thanks to football practice (and girls), Tut had slimmed down the past couple of years.

Ahead of us, we saw him swat away the brush at each turn, finally get to the creek bank, and begin to slosh across in his dress clothes instead of going to where the stream had narrowed so much that it now allowed for stepping over. Planting his right foot halfway up the bank, and using the shovel for support, he was on the ridge in three forceful steps, becoming still in the center of the deteriorating fort.

He stared at the ground, his brow furrowed with determination and a hint of disbelief.

All three cornerstones were still standing, though they were leaning at odd angles. Only tatters of the white sheets remained, a few frayed wisps were gently blowing in the light breeze of the May evening.

As we stood at the creek's edge watching, not wanting to get dirty by crossing to the other side, Tut slowly looked up at us, troubled. He was carefully working something out in his mind, hesitating; he didn't want to be wrong.

His eyes locked with mine in a long, painful moment that was years in the making. He was sheepishly asking for forgiveness.

Though I couldn't help but smile at the overdue realization, I allowed him the moment, shifted my gaze downward, nodding my understanding. Tut backed up to that old center railroad tie with its cavern still going into the earth and, lifting his right arm perpendicular to the ground as if to keep himself in a straight line, took two big steps forward before using the weight of his right foot on the shovel.

"*What* is he doing?" Lah asked loudly, exasperated, and started toward him. But I caught her arm.

We stayed on the other bank and watched as the dirt began to pile up. When the shovel eventually hit something hard, Tut worked furiously, eventually getting down on his hands and knees to feel what was there.

"It's . . . it's a box," he breathed, barely able to get the words out.

Lah and I exchanged looks, then rushed over. With focused determination, the three of us plunged our hands into the hole. It took a while, but eventually we managed to free the box from the dirt.

It was as large as an oversized shoe box, but it was metal and hinged on one side. In fact, it seemed built for rugged use, like the boxes I'd seen on television in stories about military personnel. An electric thrill ran through me, mixed with a bit of trepidation.

Lah grabbed at the box to try to open it, but Tut jerked it away from her with uncharacteristic force.

"Don't touch it," he said, his voice rough, shaking.

Hunching his shoulders, he crossed his arms over the box, protecting it. He was wild-eyed and trembling, his grip tight. A palpable tension surrounded us, thick with anticipation for whatever secrets lay within.

Backing away from us, he wiped the dirt from the top, which had been dented by the shovel. He sat there a long while trying to determine whether or not to open it, unsure what he would find. An exhilarating sense of possibility enveloped us, and as we waited, the sounds of the evening seemed to swell. The gentle trickling of the creek grew louder, mingling with the rustling leaves and distant calls of night birds. The world around us seemed to amplify, mirroring our eager curiosity. Each heartbeat felt like a countdown, and our eyes were locked on Tut, urging him silently to make a choice.

Of course, we didn't *know* that it belonged to Graduation Jesus. It could have all been a fluke.

But sometimes things just click with a surety that can't be denied. Even though it was far-fetched and surreal, we resolutely believed only Jesus could have put the box there. We felt a connection. Instead of the desertion I felt on the creek bank years ago, there was the heaviness of presence.

It was getting dark when Tut finally decided to open the box. He'd cleaned it off with his hands and was still holding it. Our parents had gradually joined us at the creek, shining flashlights, trying to figure out what was going on. After all, we'd abruptly left our own party.

With everyone looking on, Tut unclasped the latch and tugged at the top—gingerly at first and then shifting his hands to get a good grip. The dent made with the shovel had warped the shape so much that it was hard to open.

When the hinge finally yielded and with our families leaning in, Tut found himself staring into a box of baby items, including a small teddy bear, a rattle, a soft blue blanket folded tightly, and a pair of white, newborn shoes about as long as an index finger. Everything was carefully arranged.

Tucked beside the items was a handwritten note:

> *There is a river.*
> *And its streams make glad the city of God.*
> *My son plays on its banks.*
> *Aaron James Beebe*
> *(d. March 4, 1983)*

Lah's mother gasped and covered her mouth with her hand. We all turned to her, sensing the weight of her emotion.

"I remember," she said softly, pausing as if gathering her thoughts. "I remember when this child died. It was devastating. They'd struggled for so long to conceive, and then, when the baby was at full term, the umbilical cord became wrapped, and he died in the womb. The mother had to go through the pain of giving birth, knowing that her son was already gone."

I'll never forget the way Tut held that box, slowly understanding just how precious it was.

To him, I'm sure it felt as though he was holding that baby's tiny casket. For the longest time he didn't know what to do or where to place it. He was sorry then that he'd unearthed it because it was a private tragedy that had happened to Graduation Jesus for goodness' sake. It was a box of his own buried torment, not meant for us to uncover.

As Tut's fingers traced the box's surface, we all shared in the grief of a life lost before it even began. The moment felt spiritual, as if we had crossed a threshold into a realm where joy and sorrow mingled, binding us together in a shared history we never knew we had. We understood, then, that it was no accident we'd built our fort in that very place, centered over a special well of souls, near the restorative water that wound deep through the woods out to Campbell Creek Cemetery.

"Well," Tut said. "That about does it." He slapped his hands together to dust them off and stood up to survey his work.

It was a week after graduation, and, after a time of struggling to know exactly what to do, he'd directed us as we cleaned up the area where our fort had been. We dug out the concrete and removed the old, leaning supports. There, on a Saturday, we reburied the box.

Raym helped us craft a cross, modeled after those made by Dub Quincy that we'd heard about for years, and we positioned it to mark the spot, piling stones around the base. We included the very stones that had supported the fort's original three pillars, and in a way, the three of us. On the cross, we didn't include a date or a name. Instead, to signify that the area was sacred, we inscribed simply: Jehovah Shammah, or "The Lord is here."

We followed Tut's detailed instructions closely. He'd been the one who had touched the box, and it made the project personal and real. He wanted to get it right.

We stood back and surveyed our work.

It felt disrespectful not to say a few words, yet no words felt adequate. The moment, in more than one way, represented a point of closure. We were on the cusp of beginning totally new lives as we would soon be going our separate ways to different colleges—Lah to Arkansas, Tut to Mississippi, and me to Missouri.

We smelled the musky air and knew that, in spite of all the comfort of place and of each other, the reality of our impending separation loomed overhead. Each of us stood on the brink of a new chapter, while the creek murmured a quiet farewell, its gentle flow echoing our goodbyes.

As I looked at the cross that stood resolutely against the natural backdrop of the trees, I felt the importance of what we had done. The cross was more than a marker; it was a testament to our collective journey, a promise that our shared memories would remain in this space long after we had moved on. It stood as a witness, holding our laughter, tears, and the stories we had yet to tell.

Even though it was a constant summer presence, I suddenly noticed the heat of the sun. It wrapped around us, gathered us into a huddle. I felt the growing pressure to say something significant. It had just come to me to model after the poetic speech of Graduation Jesus and use the scripture from Joshua 4 to tell my two lifelong best friends that the stones we'd piled would be a memorial forever when, before I could say anything, Tut let out a snort as his stomach growled louder than any of our thoughts.

Lah collapsed into giggles.

"I could eat," Tut said, patting his stomach as I grinned and shook my head. Before we walked away, we committed to returning periodically to maintain the special area.

We never said a word to Brother Beebe. We knew he'd find the precious memorial on his own.

And it was years later before I truly worked out the weight of the experience in my mind. I was in graduate school mulling over a passage from William Goyen, a short story writer whose work I had used as the topic for a research paper.

Goyen runs thoughts together in a way that visually illustrates the process of transformation. His fluidity is purposeful. It invites the reader into the complexity of the character's experience while also emphasizing the connectedness of sorrow and redemption.

One leads to the other.

In "Author Bond," the narrator says, "... *my God the workings of Jehovah's ways, a worm to make an Angel, oh Lord why is there so much darkness in this life before we see the light of things your ways are strange your ways are dark before we see the light.*"

As I poured over Goyen's words, I found myself pondering the metamorphosis of pain into joy, reflecting on how the buried sorrows we unearthed together as teenagers had become a profound bond that sustained us through the years. Somehow it helped me to know that the torment we'd found was a worm that made an angel.

The grotesque image, a box of keepsakes some might consider morbid and unsettling, helped me understand it all really.

In making our discovery, we'd realized that every conversation we'd ever had there in our fort was larger than the three of us.

And it wasn't invasive to know we'd been surrounded by a great cloud of witnesses. There was a sense of communion.

It was as if the past and present were woven together, creating a patchwork quilt of intersecting stories. I couldn't explain it then, but—in joy, in pain, in all the sameness of life—we were connected in a way that reaches into forever, just as Jesus said.

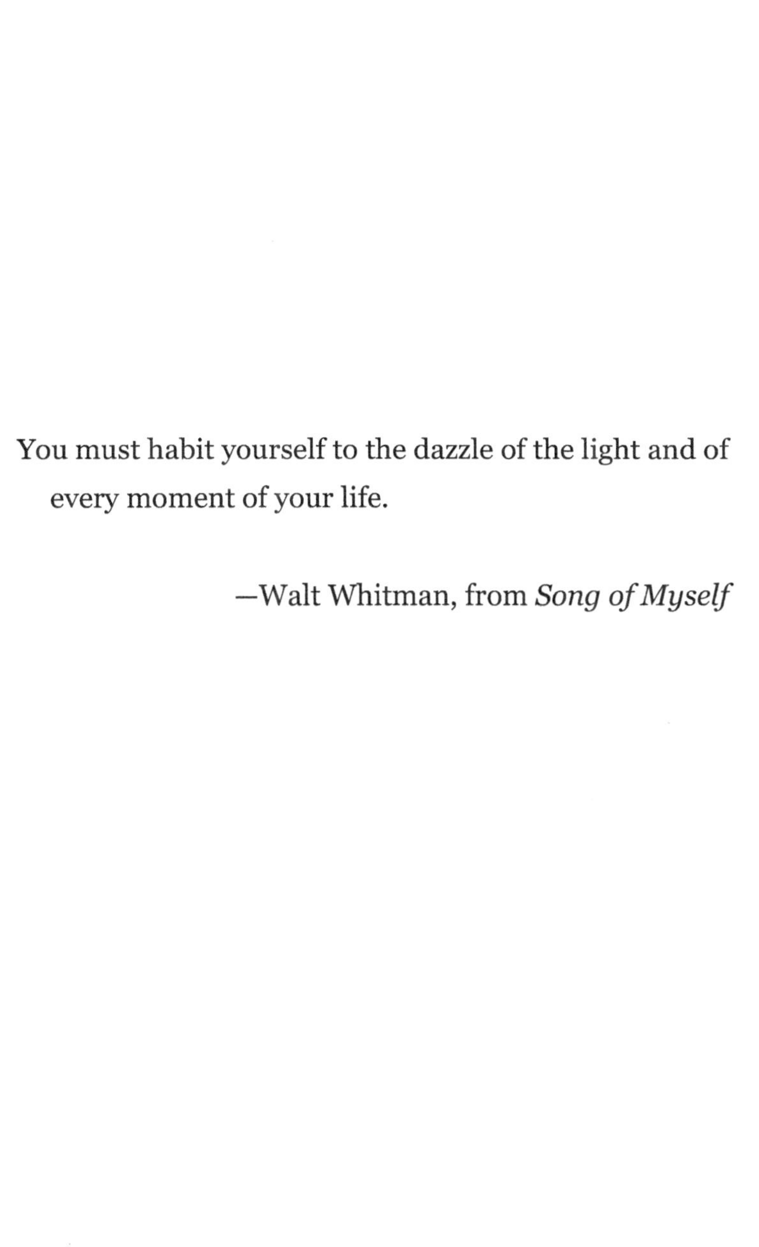

You must habit yourself to the dazzle of the light and of every moment of your life.

—Walt Whitman, from *Song of Myself*

SIX

High Potential

(1991)

Lah, Tut, and I agreed we'd spend the summer after our sophomore year together at home in Sharp, and now I'm finally on my way home. We've come back periodically, mind you. I don't mean to sound as though we've dropped off the planet somehow or that we're too far away to ever come home again. But with our various school schedules, we've struggled to coordinate our timing. We've not seen each other for more than a few days since high school.

It's been a quick two years. The quickest.

The first couple months I was away, there was no mail from home to speak of, just a regular "Miss You" or "Thinking of You" type card from our youth leader at the church. When I started noticing these always arrived on the same day, I smiled, envisioning Sister Diane sitting down every Sunday afternoon methodically checking items off the list on her clipboard. Her efforts were genuine, but there was a certain predictability to them, as if she were collecting points for each card sent. I was sure that Lah and Tut would also receive cards that day. (Sister Diane would be pleased to make three checks.)

Raym and Bingo call often. Sometimes, even Big calls. Always short check-ins asking the perfunctory questions of an older brother. He is living on his own now and working as an accountant.

Gradually, upon learning that I am studying journalism, people began sending me clippings from the *Alexandria Daily Town Talk* with any sort of news they thought I might find interesting.

There is a story that I have begun following closely, although I am too embarrassed to bring my clippings to class most days. A former grand wizard of the Ku Klux Klan is running for governor against Edwin Edwards who has already held the office for 12 years (though he'd lost the most recent election). While one might think the "news" is the Klansman, Edwards' career has been filled with racketeering charges, so his current campaign slogan is just as absurd: "Vote for the Crook. At Least He's Honest!" It's hard to believe that these are the two candidates to be offered on the upcoming ballot.

It is Louisiana though, after all.

Beyond these political stories, Bingo has been sending me the "Society" section of the *Town Talk* with just a single line highlighted in yellow here and there. These are my favorite clips.

Not long after I'd left for college, Raym decided to run for Justice of the Peace for Ward 7, and he'd been elected. He's been a Notary Public all my life, and I am accustomed to people showing up unannounced, needing him to emboss documents with his official stamp. He charges five or ten dollars (he is never consistent with it), or sometimes people bring by fresh eggs or vegetables from their garden and he doesn't charge at all. But now, he is performing marriages!

I can only imagine how surreal it must be for Raym to be entrusted with such an important role in people's lives. Bingo shares clips of wedding announcements where he's been listed as the officiant. Some announcements refer to him as the "minister," which, of course, is incorrect.

I've heard stories. And not just from Raym.

On my three-way calls with Tut and Lah each week, the news from home makes it to me passed through their families and then through them. Just like with the notary work, couples are now showing up unannounced wanting to be married on the spot. Both Tut's and Lah's parents have been called over from next door to serve as witnesses multiple times. Apparently, it's become common for anyone nearby to get asked to be a witness at a moment's notice.

The three of us laugh at the anecdotes. The brides dressed in wedding gowns driving up with grooms still in their coveralls and muddy work boots. The bevy of guests some couples have in tow, sometimes so many cars they'll have to sidle off the driveway, rutting up the yard, while others show up alone. Literally. Some brides and grooms came in separate cars, having agreed to meet up at Raym's at a certain time and go back to work afterwards.

The weddings are always interesting, and Raym enjoys them very much, but the sense of being caught unawares has gotten to be so much of an issue that he keeps a blazer downstairs on a hook behind the pantry door to throw on over his clothes.

He's also laminated a hand-printed sign that simply says, "Call before coming." It's tacked to a tree at the top of the driveway.

The sign is largely ignored.

Raym is easygoing about it as he enjoys hearing each couple's story and usually finds some connection to them (he's discovered quite a few distant cousins), but he doesn't like it when his standing date with Tom Brokaw and the *NBC Nightly News* at 5:30 p.m. is interrupted. Sometimes Bingo stops couples out on the carport and small-talks them a bit while Raym finishes watching the news before starting their vows.

This isn't appreciated in summer months—as a general rule, sweat isn't attractive—so some give a *hmph* and stomp to their vehicles to wait it out, running the AC wide open. Even Louisiana humidity can't kill the romance of a wedding though. The seemingly irritated brides and grooms step back out of their cars promptly at 6 p.m., smiling and straightening their dress clothes, ready to get hitched.

I snicker about this to myself as I check the time. It's nearing 7 p.m. I've been trying to occupy my mind for the last few hours of the trip home from Columbia. Interstate driving is very boring, but I'm thankful for it as I-49 only recently opened to Central Louisiana and the new route feels smooth and luxurious (the longer stretch from Shreveport to Lafayette is not expected to be complete until 1996).

Finally taking Exit 103 toward Sharp, the green road a glorious beacon, I am exhausted . . . and happy that I won't be arriving during the news.

I will be the last to make it home. Lah arrived yesterday, and Tut's semester ended in early May, so he's been home nearly a week. His parents have already had him busy with summer yardwork projects.

Four miles after taking the exit, I finally slow to turn right into the long driveway. The spring sun is still bright, and I'm sure the heat will hit me hard the moment I open the car door. The pea gravel beneath my tires shifts as I approach the house, the familiar sight of it instantly grounding me like I'd never left.

Ahead, I see a black Honda Accord pulled up to the carport and realize it's new. Beautifully shiny and clean with a temporary license plate taped in the back glass. Even stiff from driving over eight hours straight, I jump out excitedly—Lord knows why I think some things—assuming I'm being surprised with a brand new car.

I bound through the back door to walk in on Raym standing in front of a couple in the middle of the kitchen.

Startled, they all turn, as Bingo hurriedly walks toward me, putting a finger to her lips to say, "shhh."

Tut and Lah are sitting in barstools at the kitchen counter watching it all in amusement.

I cut eyes at them and can't find any words.

The bride and groom appear to be in their sixties. They are beaming at each other like high school sweethearts, and, with the woman sliding a ring onto the man's finger, it is apparent that the ceremony is almost over.

There is a comfortable, breezy feeling in the air, so I join Lah and Tut to watch, getting the sense that the room has been filled with laughter. Raym's blue eyes are twinkling when he pronounces them husband and wife, and they share a tender kiss that makes the three of us cheer in delight.

The couple, Nowell and Patti, stay for coffee and giggle at our gentle teasing about finally tying the knot. They've been together for 22 years. Tut serves as the first witness, and I jump ahead of Lah to be the second to sign their certificate, gleefully enjoying my first experience with the impromptu weddings I've heard about secondhand.

After they leave, Raym patiently responds to our many questions. We're eager to hear all the details about other kitchen weddings he's performed.

"Now that Big and Missy are out of the house, you should sell the pool table in the game room and set up a little chapel," Tut laughs.

Raym nods, his gaze distant. "People don't seem to mind the kitchen," he says. "I've married some on the front porch in the swing or in the front yard under the oaks. I even had one couple stand out by my tractor in the field, and then they posed with it afterward for pictures. They were dressed in jeans, boots, and cowboy hats, and they thought it made for a great, country-themed wedding. It doesn't matter where you say 'I do.' Just that you mean it."

Hours after Tut and Lah are gone, I'm still thinking about Nowell and Patti, wondering why, after so many years, they'd choose to get married this way. Was it a whim? What made them finally want to formalize what they already knew? Perhaps the absence of family and friends made their choice feel even more personal, as if the kitchen held all the significance they needed. Coming home always makes me reflective, but the seemingly impromptu wedding has given me a lot to ponder.

The first Saturday morning I'm home Bingo wakes me up at 6 a.m. to go garage saling in Alexandria (about 20 minutes away via the sweet new I-49).

"We need to be on the road within 15 minutes," she announces loudly, jerking the covers off me.

"I've marked some high potentials," she says.

Still half-asleep, I throw on jeans and a T-shirt and head downstairs to find Lah in our living room. She is wearing overall shorts with her hair in a ponytail sticking through the back of a baseball cap. I see the angled strap of her crossbody purse. She's in her battle outfit, and, seeing me, she starts walking toward the door. She is ready for action. The morning light streaming through the window casts a determined glow on her face.

"I'm driving!" I grump at them, as Bingo hands me a lidded Tupperware mug with coffee and a biscuit she's stuffed with muscadine jelly and rolled up in a paper towel.

We walk outside and I head toward my car, parked in the drive of the separate garage where Raym stores his antique cars, only to look back and see that Bingo and Lah are not with me. They've gotten into Bingo's Dodge Caravan under the carport.

With a long sigh, I turn around.

Bingo, waiting in the passenger seat, already has the *Town Talk* opened to the garage sale section. I can see the large Xs where she's crossed out the addresses she won't waste time on and the numbers she's printed next to some of the others indicating the order she wants to attack them.

As I settle in, adjusting the rearview mirror and sliding the driver's seat closer to the steering wheel, I feel Bingo's impatience but move at my own pace. I can practically hear the clock ticking louder as I fumble with my seatbelt, while Bingo taps her foot like a metronome, clearly rehearsing the ultimate eye roll for when I finally get it on. I flip through the wad of keys to find the right one, finally turning it in the ignition, and adjust the air conditioner vents before pulling napkins from her special Tupperware caddy and placing them in my lap. I unwrap my biscuit, take another sip of coffee, and rummage in my purse for lip balm, trying to ignore Bingo's growing restlessness.

90

Finally, she can't hold it anymore.

"IT'S GO TIME! GO! GO! GO!"

Grinning, I twist to look behind me and back the van out of the carport, catching Lah's laughter.

Bingo's first "high potential" is a total bust. Seeing only a few household items stacked on a makeshift plywood table and a sagging rack of clothing (a wire strung between a basketball goal and the edge of the garage), she calls an audible.

"Don't stop, don't stop," she says, shaking her left hand toward me as if her words alone aren't enough. I'd slowed down, but not yet hit the brake, so I accelerate again, and we all look straight ahead, passing the sale as if we're too dignified to stop, and we're on our way to somewhere more important.

The second "high potential" appears to be a jackpot.

It is a house on Welwyn Way in Charleston Park, one of the nicest subdivisions in Alexandria (it's curbed and guttered). A treadmill and a few upscale furniture pieces are set out in the drive—a sure sign that other good stuff is waiting to be had in the actual garage. Cars line both sides of the street at least four houses away on either side.

"I knew we should've hit this one first," Bingo complains, as if we are late. It is just after 7 a.m., and I take her comment as a direct criticism (though we are following the numbers she'd printed on the *Town Talk* ads), so I decide to pause in front of the house to drop the two of them off while I park.

A horn immediately blares. An extended blast. With cars lining both sides of the street, there's not enough room to go around us. I look into the rearview mirror to see an angry fist shaking at me. A man behind the wheel of a pickup, with two women crammed into the small cab beside him, is mouthing something. I can't catch every word, but I read his lips enough to know his comments aren't inspired by the Holy Spirit.

I motion to try to get Bingo and Lah back into the van, the irate outburst making me uncomfortable, but, always good-natured, Lah has already given the man her best grin, an overly-dramatic bow, and a wave in apology. She and Bingo are hot-trotting it to the sale.

Hurriedly getting out of the way, I continue down the street, noticing that, behind me, the truck is wedging into the first available opening at an angle. I decide to drive around the block before coming back to park.

By the time I'm back on Welwyn Way, the string of cars has grown even longer. I have to park six or eight cars away, well before I reach the house with the sale. As I step out, I notice a buzz of activity up ahead. People are moving with purpose, like they're on the verge of finding something valuable.

Joining the flow of garage salers on the sidewalk, I make my way toward the house. Ahead, I can see that the driveway is already filled with people browsing and examining items. That's when I spot him—the man from the truck—now with both arms locked around one of the treadmill's handrails, his determination as solid as the machine he's claimed. He is leaning at an angle as if bracing his feet in the driveway, lest he be carried away by force. The two women are standing nearby, staring on in disbelief at his rudeness.

"I'm sorry," a stylish, silver-haired woman says in a placating tone. She is stuffing a few dollars into a fanny pack and has a marker in her hand. It's obvious she is the homeowner and that she is overwhelmed by the horde of people, making me frown that she is alone. "Someone has just paid for it and will be back soon to pick it up. I was just about to mark it as sold."

I can see the $25 tag still hanging, a price anyone knows is too low for a working treadmill.

"It's what I came for and it's not my fault I missed it!" shrieks the vulgar-mouthed man as I rejoin Lah and Bingo. They are sifting through items on folding tables neatly aligned inside the garage, oblivious to the driveway incident. Bingo is piling Lah's arms high with used Tupperware toys.

"This one looks *absolutely brand new*," she says, incredulously, adding a Tupperware Shape-O Ball to the top of the stack.

Bingo continues to snatch all the Tupperware pieces she sees. She hands me a two-quart pitcher, and as I dangle it by the handle, I can't help but move toward the commotion, somehow feeling intimately involved. I can feel it escalating, with several garage salers making eye contact, setting down the items they'd picked up, and quietly moving on to the next sale.

The man, red-faced and now sweating through his shirt, refuses to relinquish his grip on the treadmill.

With the marker still in hand, the silver-haired woman plucks up her courage, walks closer, and repeats firmly, "It's already sold, sir. There's nothing I can do."

I'm stepping closer and closer, feeling somehow protective of her, unable to look away.

Finally sensing something off, Lah shifts her weight to one leg and looks around, clutching the stack of Tupperware toys. Bingo, on the other hand, is still too absorbed in her treasure hunt to notice.

"Is there a problem?" Lah finally calls out, her chipper voice cutting through the tension.

The vulgar-mouthed man's head snaps toward us then. His eyes narrow, and for a moment, I fear he might come charging at us violently like a raging bull.

But the vulgar-mouthed man doesn't move. He fixes upon Lah with a penetrating glare. I can feel his contempt by his stance—his anger hitting a boiling point as he stands up straight and jerks a fist onto his hip. "Mind your business," he spits. "It's all because of you, anyway!"

"It sounds like you just need a Dr. Pepper," Lah snarks, with raised eyebrows and an exaggerated sympathetic tone. A mischievous smile is playing on her lips.

"No need to get ugly over a piece of exercise equipment. We all know you're just buying it to resell anyway," she says.

Bingo finally looks up then, her eyes widening as she takes in the scene. "Lah!" she mutters. "You're gonna start something."

But it's too late. The man's face flushes an even deeper shade of crimson. He moves to step away from the treadmill, and for a second, it seems like the world holds its breath. My heart is beating in my ears. I can hear the silence we all make, not one of us budging an inch, not even in the dread of what's to come.

Then, instead of moving toward us, with a roar, he kicks the rail of the treadmill, knocking it on its side and slamming it hard against the concrete driveway. He continues kicking it, and, suddenly seeing the power cord, grabs it with both hands, yanking it out of the unit so hard that it flies into the air like a whip that has been cracked, snapping back up in a wild arc.

"There!" he shouts, his chest heaving. "Nobody gets to use it now!"

The silver-haired woman gasps, her hand flying to her mouth, and I instinctively step forward, not sure what I can do, but ready to intervene if necessary.

I notice Lah's movement just in time to catch her arm. She is poised with the Shape-O ball raised, ready to hurl it at the vulgar-mouthed man.

"Not the Shape-O ball!" I scream. "Bingo will kill us!"

Before I can say anything else, a different voice cuts through the commotion.

"What is going on here? Bev, you OK?"

It's a gravelly voice, full of quiet authority.

We turn to see a man, probably in his mid-seventies, making his way up the driveway supporting himself with a cane. His steady gait and calm demeanor suggest someone used to being taken seriously.

The vulgar-mouthed man takes one look at the newcomer and deflates like a punctured balloon.

Even angry, a Southerner always respects his elders.

He mutters something under his breath, but it's clear he's lost whatever fight he has left. Without another word, he slinks away, starts walking toward his truck, the two women glaring daggers at him and slowly following.

The older man, who I assume to be the silver-haired woman's husband, steps up to the treadmill, inspecting the damage with a sigh.

"Can't believe there would be such a fuss over a treadmill," he says, shaking his head.

Bev gives him a relieved smile. "Thank you, Harold," she whispers, patting his arm.

"Well, garage saling sure is eventful," Lah quips, relieved the situation has diffused. Bingo cracks a smile as I notice all the other garage salers are gone, leaving just the three of us.

Harold spies the pile of Tupperware toys in Lah's arms. "Y'all find anything worth taking home?" he asks, his mouth twitching into a grin.

Bingo, ever the negotiator, doesn't miss a beat. "These are for the church toddlers," she says, holding up a TupperCanoe like a trophy. "If you're looking to make a deal, I'm all ears."

Harold chuckles, the sound deep and warm. "For the church, huh? Well, in that case, you can take the lot for a dollar. Those toys belonged to our grandkids, but they're all grown up now."

Bingo's face lights up, and she digs into her purse. With a flourish, she produces a $20 dollar bill and insists that he take it.

Lah tilts her head at Harold. "You got any more treasures hiding in there?"

"Just some fishin' gear," he replies, with a wink. "But you don't strike me as the fishin' type."

"You'd be surprised," Lah retorts, her tone playful.

As we walk toward the van, I glance back at the driveway. The treadmill lies abandoned, a casualty of the morning's excitement. It's such a silly thing—something no one wanted until someone else claimed it.

The summer slipped by in a series of humid days, punctuated by the weddings Raym officiated that cropped up like wildflowers—unexpected, colorful, and a bit unruly. Each one was different, yet they all carried the same vibrant thread of spontaneity and sincerity that left me mulling over how I myself would quantify words like "love" and "commitment," if asked.

There was the giddy young couple who'd driven from Natchitoches, a college town about thirty minutes north. They couldn't have been more than 20 years old. The bride had insisted on wearing her grandmother's wedding dress, a delicate thing that looked ready to disintegrate in the Louisiana heat. They'd wanted to marry where no one knew them, to keep the day just for themselves, and Raym had obliged. They left our kitchen looking like they'd just stepped out of *Gone With the Wind*, her train sweeping up the dust from the floor.

Then there was the pair, much older than Raym and Bingo, from just down the road in Flatwoods. They'd been together for nearly 50 years, and the man had finally proposed after surviving a heart attack.

"Figured it was about time," he'd said, grinning at Raym. He was still weak, the aftereffects of his health scare evident, and his hands trembled slightly as he slid the ring onto his bride's finger. Raym had to rush the ceremony, so that the groom could sit down and rest. It was a poignant reminder that life's fragility makes every moment we share together that much sweeter.

They'd stayed for lunch, telling Lah, Tut, and me stories about the old days, their laughter punctuating each memory. Their tales wove a colorful mosaic of shared experiences. They left us feeling like we'd been given a glimpse into a world where love wasn't rushed, but ripened over decades.

Two paramedics had come to be married in their uniforms, driving an ambulance. The bride, looking exhausted, held their newborn baby during the ceremony—which Raym had to pause so that she could step aside to change a diaper. Their vows were simple and direct, and they drove off in the ambulance, lights off, no sirens, without so much as a honeymoon planned, just a promise to finish what they'd started.

By the time August rolled around, I'd seen more kitchen weddings than I'd ever imagined, each one a little universe of its own. There was something about the way the couples stood before Raym, no frills or fancy decorations, just the bare bones of a ceremony to mark their devotion, that made me think about what it meant to find "high potential" in a person. It wasn't about the probability of future success or some agenda they hoped to fulfill. It was about the unspoken belief that they could build something meaningful together, day by day, through moments that others might overlook.

The weddings Raym officiated that made it into the "Society" section now seem like hollow affairs, with plastic smiles and staged photos, compared to the genuine simplicity of these home ceremonies. My journalistic mind always prefers a narrative rich with truth over one polished to appear perfect.

As I think about the upcoming semester, I know I'll be asked about the controversial political landscape in my home state, especially the embarrassing governor's race. I struggle to decide how to approach it. Both candidates appear to be putting on a show, much like the "Society" pieces, presenting a façade that belies the deeper issues at play.

Then, there's the lottery story. Last fall, on October 6, 1990, voters approved a constitutional amendment creating the Louisiana Lottery, intended to generate much-needed revenue without raising taxes. The funds are meant to support public education, making it a compelling topic for my assignments, especially since Missouri's own lottery was only approved a few years earlier, in 1986. The undercurrent of greed and desperation among ticket buyers grasping at the hope of sudden wealth give me pause though. For every winner celebrated, there are throngs of others who will never see a return on their investment, holding scraps of paper that symbolize nothing but lost aspirations. On the surface, the lottery appears to be a positive economic development, but lurking beneath is a deeper, more troubling reality that raises questions about the true cost of those fleeting dreams.

As I pack my bags for the trip back to Missouri, my thoughts drift away from possible topics for political or current events assignments and toward the people I'd watched say "I do." What stands out isn't just their devotion; it's their willingness to face uncertainty head-on, to step into something they know can unravel at any moment but that they believe is worth the risk.

It isn't always beautiful. In fact, often, it's downright messy. I think about the couple who got married with their newborn between them. Nothing screams "life's not a fairy tale" like having to pause your own wedding to change a diaper. The baby's cries, the unmistakable stench hanging in the air, the parents' tired faces—that is real life, unfolding in all its chaotic glory. No one was concerned about the smell or the interruption though. It was as if the diaper change was just another part of the day, as natural as the vows they exchanged.

Maybe that's what makes the kitchen weddings so much more convincing than the polished affairs I see celebrated in print, with their glossy photos and perfectly crafted descriptions.

Life doesn't wait for perfection.

There's no promise that everything will be neat and tidy, and maybe that's what it's all about—finding treasure in the ordinary, recognizing the value in what others might overlook, and choosing to make it yours. Maybe that's enough.

On my last night at home, after everyone else has gone to bed, I pull out the fortune cookie slip I've been carrying around in my wallet the past few months. It reads, *Look at life through a new lens and you'll discover hidden treasures.*

It had felt like a nice sentiment when I first got it, but now, after a summer of watching couples find something precious in each other, it holds a deeper meaning.

As I lay awake, I think of Nowell and Patti, Harold and Bev, and all the other couples I've met.

When I finally begin the long drive to school, my mind is crowded with fresh ideas. Looking ahead to my journalism classes, I am full of new stories to tell.

Clear and sweet is my soul, and clear and sweet is all
that is not my soul . . . I am satisfied—I see, dance,
laugh, sing . . .

—Walt Whitman, from *Song of Myself*

SEVEN

The Great Schism

(1993)

I am 22 years old and a senior at the University of Missouri. Home is 695 miles south and, at times, it is difficult to remember why I have chosen to be alone and away from all that I know. I very much miss the grand oaks that framed and calmed my youth, serving as a canopy over my life.

I even miss Boo Boo the cat, though it's been ten years now since he passed away.

Perhaps it is the impending conclusion of my college years, being on the cusp of turning away from one season of life to begin anew, that has me in a profound state of retrospection. I find myself deeply entrenched within a compilation of time where past and present are fused together. My memories of growing up in Sharp remain unusually vividly and alive—especially incidents with Raym, Bingo, Big, Tut, Lah, and my crazy Aunt Mackie. I exist in a mental realm where things simply *are* and always will be.

Interestingly, the rumination serves me well. These memories, in fact, are what I use for content and context in my academic life.

I am a proud student at the Missouri School of Journalism, considered among professionals to be the best journalism school in the United States. Students here are unabashedly and discriminately screened, with those making the cut being put immediately to work in various campus and local media. I was initially made a staff writer for the *Columbia Missourian*, a daily morning newspaper published entirely by students.

My first two years at the university and at the *Missourian* were spent as a beat reporter covering the meetings of the Columbia City Council. Beats are typically staid and boring assignments, but at that time, there was a downtown revival effort underway. The council was pushing to extend Elm Street, build a state-of-the-art performing arts center, connect the university's campus to downtown shopping areas, and further develop the Biscayne Mall. And, all of these proposed developments were promoted with the teaser that they would be "green" initiatives.

Though the residents wanted to do what was right for the environment, using sustainable building materials and saving trees by choosing alternative (and longer) routes for new streets more than doubled the development costs. The city just couldn't afford it, and what the council had thought would be leverage to politic for ardent support to *build* turned into an angry backlash to *stop*. Combine this with the scandal over the traffic trap of fining residents $300 for short-cutting through the parking lot of Patricia's Flower Shop to avoid the red light on the corner of Broadway and North Keene, the debate over using city funds to help renovate the historic Tiger Hotel, and the constant special requests of the First Baptist Church (an outfit so big, many referred to it as Six Flags Over Jesus), and, well, I stayed busy.

It was hard not to take sides on the issues I covered. However, neutrality is the test of the beat reporter, so for two years, I stuck to the facts only, sometimes almost robotically. The journalistic process had been thoroughly hammered into me. Even in social conversation, I tended to sift through small talk and summarize events into a who, what, when, where, why matrix in my head, sloughing off trivial details and focusing on the "why," which was what mattered most—at least to me.

My junior year I was promoted to more fun and creative projects. It was the school's typical maturing method: two years of laborious practice in basic reporting before moving into feature writing. The intent was to ensure journalists had been honed into professionals before turning them loose with subjects that were potentially controversial or emotionally charged.

My classmates were assigned college sports, local crime, financial trends, and even politics to introduce their judgement skills in selecting story angles. Surprisingly, though, I was assigned "Small-Town Stories," a special series of features where I traveled to the tiny communities on the outskirts of Columbia to interview all the Aunt Verties and Uncle Buddys who grew the largest watermelons, produced two- and three-yolk eggs, and saw UFOs on clear nights.

I wasn't sure why I was given the opportunity to craft full-blown exposés that allowed for nostalgia and scenery and personality while my classmates' features were in-depth analyses of topics like the current mortgage interest rate and its projected rise and fall or the problem of overcrowding in the city jail, but it certainly suited me.

In the small towns I covered, I had the same feeling I did growing up in rural, central Louisiana. I was in a comfort zone rare for my age and never hesitated to write about topics such as the raffling of quilts sewn by the Eastern Star ladies while my classmates investigated religious wars in foreign countries. Something in me knew that my stories were equally important; those quilts had seen their own wars. I understood the treasures the quilts would become and the heritages they upheld.

As I became more immersed in these communities, I also became connected to the people whose stories I told, cheering for each hometown victory, each hard-earned agricultural feat. I clapped for every hog, chicken, or cow raised and shown at county fairs by the FFA or 4-H club. I ate the first dense pancakes prepared by Mrs. Conley's sophomore home economics class. I tacked up posters for lost dogs, bake sale fundraisers, and Christmas food drives. Oh, the people I met!

I covered my share of more serious stories, too. I helped mourn the loss of a town's native son, a tragedy that came in a wasteful accident after a Friday night football game.

And some stories haunted me.

Like the time the community rallied around Tim and Rebecca Johnson. Their toddler's heart surgery went perfectly, and then while the family rejoiced in relief, an unexpected complication caused sudden death in the recovery room, an awful twist of fate. I was there when that grieving mom walked out and told those of us waiting how she had held her two-year-old son's lifeless body, and struggling to even breathe, looked up through the ceiling to the beyond and said, ". . . OK, God" in horrible surrender to the reality she hated but could not change.

But there was also laughter.

Jim Vaughan was an 82-year-old farmer whose thumbs were always purple from shelling purple hull peas. His grandson had gotten him hooked on browsing the internet.

Of course, the internet was still very new to all of us, but Jim was especially suspicious. He was convinced that he should whisper his email address to me, lest anyone nefarious should overhear it. In addition to peas, Jim grew Vidalia onions and liked to demonstrate how he slept with his arms stretched wide to put as much distance as possible between his nose and the smell. He also made me rethink any time I threw something away.

Jim often joked that his rural upbringing had made him resourceful. He believed everything could be repurposed and had many examples of thriftiness, such as cutting threadbare sheets down the middle, flipping the two halves, and resewing them.

"Good as new," he would say.

Most of my fellow journalism students were from the South; some were even raised in the most rural areas of Missouri and Arkansas. It's just that they had already detached themselves from the community-centered life depicted in my stories. While I tried to capture the identity and authenticity of the people in each small town, my peers were busy running from that very thing, eager to escape the spotlight of being known by everyone.

The truth was that there wasn't a single story I hadn't already heard while writing the "Small-Town Stories" series—though the names of the characters were different, of course.

So as I publicized a spaghetti supper to be held in conjunction with the Steampunk Festival in Bolivar (a fundraiser for the new animal shelter there), and as I gently shed light on the vandalism at the high school in Harg (which was only two boys jimmying a cracked window to get into the cafeteria to steal some cookies), I relived stories I'd heard all my life when the cast of characters was Raym, his older sister Mackie, and his two older brothers Tommy and Burel.

But they weren't stories to Raym. They just *were*.

Like . . . there was the time 15-year-old Burel went with Brother O'Quinn, a deacon from the church, on a Saturday run to Ruston, Louisiana, to get a truckload of peaches. Ruston was known for its peaches, and they were a great fundraiser. It had become common and expected for a truck, loaded with baskets of peaches, to be parked in front of the church, even during services. The deacons would keep an eye trained to ensure that no peaches went missing and, of course, they'd have to step out and make a few sales as well.

It was, after all, money for the Lord.

That Saturday, when Burel and Brother O'Quinn were nearly back home from Ruston, they came upon a fatal wreck in a notoriously difficult curve on Old Highway 1. Brother O'Quinn pulled the loaded-down pickup off the road, so that he and Burel could kneel beside the wrecked vehicle to pray.

It wasn't a story to them then. It just *was*. And as I drafted my final feature assignment about the split of the First Baptist Church in Sapp, Missouri (due to the pastor's charismatic intimations), I couldn't help but think about the 1952 split of Sharp United Pentecostal Church.

Sharp UPC appeared to be the average humble country church—a white frame building with a center aisle and long, wooden pews on either side. It had a covered porch across the front, windows spaced symmetrically down the sides, and two steps leading up to a simple wooden door. The roof was tin, and a modest cross arose from atop it, centered and positioned toward the front just above the entryway. It was very unassuming.

In actuality, however, it was quite a progressive church. Pentecostalism itself was still in its infancy as the apostolic or "Holiness" movement had only taken off a few years before with the merger of two evangelical denominations. But it wasn't just that the church was Pentecostal. What made the Sharp UPC dramatically more contemporary from most churches at that time was that the elected pastor was a *woman*. It was unheard of.

In those years, there were only three things that could divide a church: an argument over the pastor; an argument over how to spend the tithes; or an argument over the music (the most important part of a Pentecostal service). Sharp UPC experienced all three at once.

It was the perfect storm.

In 1951, the church purchased a brand-new Kimball spinet organ, at great expense, to replace the Baldwin vacuum tube model that was in disrepair and no longer used. It was the very first Kimball (a highly prestigious brand) anywhere in the region.

Indeed, it was such a showpiece that visitors from other churches often attended services just to see it in action. High-dollar, long-term instruments such as this had to be considered carefully as the church members would need to seek the Lord and then vote on whether to establish a "music fund" to pay for it in the same manner as a "building fund," very common in those days.

Seeing the Kimball was a treat for those visiting, and boy did they get a show! Mackie (the same mischievous Mackie who often caught her titty in her accordion and drew "little peters" for fun) was at the center of it all. It seemed that Mackie and her friend, Sevella, both 16, were equally talented. They had grown up in the church together and started at a young age taking turns directing the worship music.

Most people in that day, especially Pentecostals, played music by ear; it was an old-style music centered on chording that translated to just about any instrument. Most anyone who could play the piano could also play the organ and guitar. Visitors were delighted by Mackie and Sevella, who were now able to lead the service's music together—one on the piano, the other on the organ.

The problem was that, even though the two were friends, they couldn't help but turn the service into a competition, each one trying to outdo the other and steal the show. Though they were supposed to take turns, the one on the Kimball always had the advantage because the volume could be ramped up to add extra drama to Sister Jarrell's sermon by inserting little "Ah-ha," "Yes, Lord," and "Amen" type notes to go along with her phrasing.

With the new organ, the notes could be drawn out, held extra-long, or raised and lowered in volume for emphasis. And, during the altar service, Mackie and

Sevella could work the crowd into a frenzy by driving the music louder and wilder.

Amid all the shouting and seeking, no one would even notice when Mackie, with a sly sideways grin to Raym, would throw in a few runs of some "boogie woogie" or a Red Foley song like "Down Yonder" without missing a beat.

Raym always sat close to the front on the organ side so that he and Mackie could conspire.

Even as a child, he understood the emotion and cadence of the service and knew when to give a signal that said, "Do it, Mackie!" His favorite was when she hit it quick in between verses of a hymn with something like, *"he pops a boogie woogie rag the Chattanooga shoeshine boy"* and then jumped right back into "Jesus I'll Never Forget" or "I'll Fly Away."

With one run and a proud grin from Mackie, Raym would jump and double over in glee.

Eventually, the competition between the two musicians got out of hand. The music began to domineer the service and the pastor couldn't preach a word without Mackie or Sevella ad-libbing and taking it too far, extending every few words with background chords. Each seemed to escalate the other's performance, creating a chaotic symphony of rivalry.

One couldn't play a single note without the other chiming in. And the congregation, caught between amusement and frustration, shifted uneasily in their pews, unsure whether to laugh or pray.

When stern looks stopped working, Sister Jarrell called out the girls in the middle of a service.

"Mu . . . si . . . cians," she said slowly and firmly. "Now it's time for the WORD," making sure to accentuate her point with a look and a nod to the parents of both girls.

The two sets of parents were smiling and fanning and absorbedly rocking back and forth in their pews to the music and preaching when, suddenly, they realized the rest of the congregation had gotten the pastor's intent and were staring at them.

And with that, every cardboard funeral fan stopped, and it was on.

The girls' parents respected the pastor, but they also sided with their daughters. A church business meeting was set for the next Sunday afternoon.

Instead of taking turns at the different services or continuing to play the services together, it was decided that it would be best for the full congregation to vote on who they wanted as the official organ player—Mackie or Sevella—and to let someone new play the piano to keep the peace (just about everyone in the congregation could play).

It was the accepted process. Anytime the church had a conflict, the members voted to decide a resolution.

But it wasn't as easy as a vote this time. How could the congregation choose between two teenage girls who were loved by everyone? Both girls' families were active in the church. Mackie's father had allowed members to run tabs at his general store (forgiving more debt than he could afford to) and had been a Sunday School teacher for years. Sevella's mother had coordinated children's activities, including Vacation Bible Schools.

The girls themselves also helped out, working in the church nursery and anywhere else needed, in addition to the time they put into the service music. So when it came time to vote, the congregation was pretty equally divided.

The two sides began politicking against one another, touting which girl was better suited for the job, and tensions grew over the pastor's involvement as well. The Mackie side believed that a male pastor would not have called the girls or their parents out publicly, embarrassing them. This caused criticism about Sister Jarrell to snowball.

Insults were hurled about how she had accepted free cardboard fans imprinted with the logo of a local business which, in turn, led to questioning of her other decisions as pastor and her competence in the role overall. Even though Sister Jarrell had served as pastor for more than four years with full support of the members, complaints at the business meeting kept escalating.

Things got out of hand quick.

Four hours later, when no compromise could be reached, it was finally and regretfully decided that the church would split. The two newly-created, smaller churches would share the building and have services at different times. The Sevella side would have access to the church from Thursday mornings at 7 a.m. until Sunday afternoons at 2 p.m. to come and go as they pleased. The Mackie side would take over the church at 2 p.m. on Sundays, temporarily holding their main weekly service on Sunday nights.

Sister Jarrell was voted out.

Sharing the church facilities seemed like a fair plan, but imagine an old, wood-frame building with no air conditioning in the Louisiana summer heat.

By necessity, the services were held with open windows, and now, with the added tension of the recent arguments, there were often members of the "other church" waiting outside, leaning in to listen, sometimes even snickering at what they heard. It was a constant reminder of the division.

With no elected pastor, the deacons alternated preaching the services, some with much more success than others. And, they especially analyzed one another's music, the pride of any Pentecostal service.

One Sunday, when the Sevella side was in the middle of a service, Sister Melba Rice, a portly saint in her late sixties who believed in raising the roof with no consideration for tone or tune, was up to sing a special and play her guitar.

She believed the most important thing was to give her all when she sang to the Lord. With one foot propped up on a rung of a wooden chair to help support her guitar, Sister Melba began her musical intro and then reared back to get a good breath and sing . . .

At the dissonant sound, the Mackie side began leaning in at every window. They rolled their eyes and made faces at each other so much that they couldn't help it anymore and started laughing loudly, causing a disruption to the service. Those in the pews had been pretending not to notice, but they now started looking around, fidgeting, wanting to stop the singing and call for order.

Sister Melba just sang louder.

Soon, Brother Bernie, one of the older deacons outside who wasn't wearing his hearing aids and didn't realize that he was being too loud, turned to his wife, slapped his leg, and asked, "You thank she's 'bout to yodel, babe?"

Brother Bernie was leaning in the first window nearest to the parking lot when he said this. Brother Carl, Sister Melba's husband, happened to be outside and was just coming in from making a sale at the peach truck and overheard it.

It broke loose then.

Brother Carl could handle the mocking and the eye-rolling because he was just as guilty of that. *Who hadn't mocked the way apostolics sing and pray?* But when Brother Bernie went so far as to use the word "yodel" to refer to his wife's singing, Brother Carl got the reds. That was making it personal.

He dove at Brother Bernie, taking his legs out from under him. The pair rolled around in the gravel, with several of the deacons outside as well as Raym, Tommy, and Burel jumping in trying to break them up.

Meanwhile, the music from inside the church continued to grow louder and louder.

Sister Melba was just pulling the pin out of her hair, allowing it to swing even with her knees, when all of a sudden, Raym screamed out as he watched Burel dive into the building through one of the open windows. Tommy had tried to hold him back, but a boy from the Sevella side had been squinching his nose at Burel, and when he saw that Brother Carl had attacked Brother Bernie, Burel decided it was the right time to get even.

At this, Mackie got the idea that they didn't have to listen to Sister Melba and her guitar any longer.

Mackie brought out her accordion and started up right there in the parking lot. Anybody knows a Pentecostal can't resist singing. Or a good Jericho March.

She belted out just two words that humbled and silenced the crowd.

Precious Lord . . .

The "outside church" immediately fell in line, answering her with the next phrase of the beloved song.

Take my hand . . .

It was as if Mackie had given a call to worship. Indeed, it was a very mature thing for her to do, an action wise beyond her years, because those outside became orderly and solemn, joining together to continue the well-known hymn.

Lead me on, let me stand,
I'm tired, I'm weak, I'm worn;
Through the storm, through the night,
Lead me on to the light,
Take my hand precious Lord,
Lead me home.

As they sang, the "outside church" began circling the building, and the "inside church" fired back. The Sevella side stood in small huddles peering out from the different windows, joining in the singing to help Sister Melba, who was now working on verse three of "The Eastern Gate."

Keep your lamps all trimmed and burning,
For the Bridegroom watch and wait;
He'll be with us at the meeting,
Just inside the Eastern Gate.

Just as the Sevella side was singing about meeting up in Heaven and Jesus being there to welcome all who may come, the church doors opened briefly and Burel was shoved back outside, his lip bloodied.

Mackie stopped. Seeing Burel, her little brother, she was incensed. Knowing she had full control of the "outside church," she motioned for the group to flank the building.

Pretty soon there were people crowded on both sides of each window in a duel of songs. The outside church continued:

When my way grows drear,
Precious Lord linger near;
When my life is almost gone,
Hear my cry, hear my call,
Hold my hand lest I fall;
Take my hand, precious Lord,
Lead me home.

A few windows snapped shut, but not many were willing to give up the light breeze to win.

The battle would've carried on indefinitely, except that it was nearing 2 p.m., which meant that it was time for the church building to be turned over. As aggravated as both sides were, they were still civil in most ways.

Slowly those inside the church gathered up their things and began to file out, singing the whole way and glaring at the opposing members that used to be their friends. Sister Melba, now walking in stocking feet and carrying her lace-up shoes and guitar, even got on to Brother Carl for taking it so far as to tussle on the ground.

"*For Heaven's sake, Carl,*" she said, completely exasperated, as she helped him dust off his clothes and look for the comb that had fallen out of his pocket.

"This is the church house!"

The switching back and forth between the two churches went on for months before someone got tired of it and jokingly mentioned that their side should just "take the church." They meant *take over* the church by changing the locks, and generally being difficult by not returning the building to the other side at the appropriate time.

But the comment triggered the outlandish idea that they could *take the church*—literally. Being a pier and beam building, it was possible. And it was not too unusual to see a building being towed down the road to a new location.

The question became—which side owned the building?

Rumors began to fly and before long there were conspiracy theories surfacing about different plots to move the church during the middle of the night. Instead of signing up on the shared schedule to be at the church to fulfill a few hours of the 24-hour prayer chain, a tradition that had not been broken since 1921 (even during the recent split), the "schedule" was now used for covert surveillance. Each side guarded the church against the other, unwilling to budge in their stance regarding the split.

A few of the more zealous deacons tucked a shotgun off in the corner while they knelt at the altar to pray. Whispers of someone sneaking off with the communion table or dismantling the pulpit to remove it in the dead of night even made the rounds, heightening everyone's nerves.

Tensions were so high that Sister Jarrell, always diplomatic, finally suggested a peaceful vote to see which side held the majority. Even though she wasn't the pastor anymore, she was still called on in a pinch.

A joint business meeting was set.

The following Sunday, promptly at 2 p.m., both sides entered the church and parted left and right, like guests at a wedding representing the families of the bride and groom. Anxiety hung thick in the air as the congregants took their places, eyeing each other warily. Joe Hilger, justice of the peace, was on hand to take the official count, and it had been predetermined that the majority would claim ownership of the building.

But just before votes were cast, he matter-of-factly announced that the Sevella side had found a separate building they would use for events in conjunction with the sanctuary itself if they were to win the vote.

The Mackie side gasped at the revelation, their disbelief palpable. Not one word had been mentioned about new and better facilities. This was guerilla warfare! As one side smiled smugly, the other fumed, feeling blindsided by the unexpected twist. When the vote was taken, the Mackie side could only watch as a few deserters were swayed by the novelty and comfort of the new location, their loyalty crumbling under the allure of fresh beginnings.

<u>Final Count</u>
Sevella Side: 86
Mackie Side: 69

Justice of the Peace Hilger had no sooner announced the result of the vote, which all had already agreed would be accepted with no argument or discussion, when humble old Brother Wooley tapped his cane against the wooden floor and stood slowly and quietly from one of the back pews.

He waited for everyone's attention before he spoke.

"Mr. Hilger, deacons, church members . . ." he looked around as if considering who else he might address by name in his speech. His gaze lingered on the faces he'd known for decades, etched with lines of weariness and concern.

"I've been a member of this church for more than 35 years. I was here even before we were Pentecostal. My wife has gone on to be with the Lord, buried down the road at our own Campbell Creek Cemetery, but my children and now my grandchildren are members here. I've never said a cross word to any of you, though I think the last few months we've all acted foolishly."

Some members began to hang their heads as if embarrassed; others were nodding in agreement.

"Well, anyway, to me, the church is more about this location than the building itself. I am more tied to the land where our families have met to worship and sing and have cookouts than I am to any building. I just wanted to say that if the other side takes the church—the building, mind you—which I understand they have been awarded, our side still owns the land, and we don't want one single tree branch harmed when the building is moved."

Brother Wooley sat down. There was silence for a long while. After all the warring of the previous months, nothing remained to be said. The weight of his words tarried, heavy in the room. It felt as if the sanctuary walls themselves were slowly absorbing everyone's unspoken thoughts. Both sides left churning ideas about how to move the frame building from its cozy space nestled beneath the trees.

Talk of the particulars filled the community. A few deacons met to work up plans, which looked like football plays sketched by a coach.

They gathered around tables, markers in hand, drawing up strategies that felt almost like battle plans. Most homes in Sharp did have a telephone at this time, but with party lines and just about everyone guilty of listening in on others' phone calls, rumors abounded. Stories morphed and turned, growing in size and importance with each retelling, and soon, it felt as if people for miles away were waiting on the edge of their seats for moving day.

In fact, the hype grew so quickly that a local television station was called. Raym, 10 years old at the time, waited at home in front of the TV for KALB to run the story of a church split so fierce that one side had agreed to take the building and the other side keep the land.

And so, early the following Saturday morning, with television cameras rolling and reporters on the scene, Mackie seized her moment.

Wearing her best dress and with her hair piled up in a baggy bun (what the little girls called the "dirty diaper do"), she pumped her accordion and led the crowd in singing as the deacons of the Sevella church placed ladders to climb atop the building and beat the tin roof down with large sledge hammers.

They beat and measured and beat and measured until they were assured that, as promised, it would pass just below the tree branches. The rhythmic thudding of the hammers echoed throughout the community, accentuating the bizarre day's atmosphere with a sense of determination.

The move was slow as the building was literally rolled out of its position on logs. Each time it was inched forward, the logs in back had to be brought to the front by hand. The effort required was monumental, a test of teamwork and resolve, with the deacons of the winning faction working together to accomplish what seemed nearly impossible. It was a massive undertaking.

But it was a victorious day for both sides.

Before long, with the church in a grotesque position in the background, nearing the road and moving so slowly as to be almost imperceptible, and with Brother Sherman Martin riding on top to beat down any places they'd missed, a picnic lunch was being served in the space where the building had rested for nearly 41 years.

Families laid out blankets and baskets of food, slowly beginning to chatter among themselves just as they always had. A few members of the Sevella side even stayed to enjoy the fellowship, unable to acknowledge the finality of the split. Some cast glances at the empty space like they were waiting for the ground to speak.

The smell of fried chicken and potato salad almost masked the strangeness of the scene, as laughter mingled with the faint creaking of the church inching along behind them.

Soon, only stacked cinderblocks remained, marking where the corners of the building had been; children used them as tables for their meal. They giggled and played, unaware of the full significance of the day. It was a reminder that life, despite its upheavals, continued.

Brother O'Quinn was there peddling peaches.

The Great Schism happened and I'm telling it to you just like Raym lived it, though it may seem more like fiction than truth.

Even I, a sympathetic writer of "Small-Town Stories" for the *Missourian*, cannot adequately relay the wonder of it all as it happened then.

Though I bet it was just life to those living it, the story seems miraculous now when one knows its full extent, knows what came next and what stories this one story enabled.

Likewise, as I interview members of the First Baptist Church in Sapp, Missouri, to complete my last college writing assignment before graduation, it is clear that they do not see the split as a story. It just *is*.

Only in hindsight will the split prove to be wistful. *To endure.*

As I prop myself up in my bed to write with my overweight Himalayan smacking little kissing noises beside me, I'm alone in apartment 232 of building H of the on-campus apartments of the University of Missouri, but I can hear my Aunt Mackie's voice in the eternality of memory.

She's there with her accordion leading a congregation in "Precious Lord."

A young Raym is there too. I see him signal, "Do it, Mackie!" and then giggle in pure joy when she pops in a few "boogie woogie" runs on the organ while in the middle of a charismatic worship song.

I am in awe of this generation, so pure, so different from my own. They provide me with so many stories to tell. There's something about those who march through this life steadfast . . . singing.

Gracious! I can tell you about some people like that.

I bequeath myself to the dirt to grow from the
     grass I love,
If you want me again look for me under your
     boot-soles.

You will hardly know who I am or what I mean,
But I shall be good health to you nevertheless,
And filter and fibre your blood.

Failing to fetch me at first keep encouraged,
Missing me one place search another,
I stop somewhere waiting for you.

—Walt Whitman, from *Song of Myself*

EIGHT

MOIALT

(1995)

Mackie's eyes were closed when Lah and I approached the bed. An IV in her withered arm was the only source of sustenance she'd had for weeks, and Raym had prepared us on a call the day before that she was fading fast. She hadn't spoken much in the past few days.

Bingo was in the room with Raym, and they quietly stood up to greet us, bracing us both in a sort of awkward side hug as we all looked down at her together. There was a man standing stiffly on the far side of the bed. He was holding a large Bible and looked uncomfortable.

"The girls are here," Raym gently spoke into Mackie's left ear.

"Missy stopped in Fayetteville to pick up Lah and they drove in from school together. They just got in," he said.

I am now in graduate school, still at the University of Missouri. Lah is working as a development officer for the Alzheimer's Association while she completes her master's in social work and waits on Ben, her fiancé, to finish his doctorate in poultry science at the University of Arkansas in Fayetteville, where they both attend.

Yes, poultry science is an official degree program, though I find that I can't say it very seriously. Studies focus on research on parasitology, virology, breeding, and genetics as well as poultry enterprise operations. Ben grew up in the industry, coming from a family of chicken farmers, and it can be quite lucrative. He actually toured Lah and me around his family plant in East Texas once. It was an impressive outfit, but I still silently repent and ask for forgiveness every time I drive through a Chick-fil-A.

Lah and I have been about two and a half hours apart through these college years. We've remained closer than sisters, but, sadly, our relationship with Tut has waned some—simply due to distance as he attended the University of Southern Mississippi and chose to stay in Hattiesburg after graduation. We occasionally still have our three-way calls. Things seem different with him though as he now has girlfriends, not girl friends.

Tut has slimmed up over the years. With his football player build, perfect teeth, and clear skin, he's something of a catch. He works as a commercial construction project manager and is in the process of serving as his own contractor to build his first personal home. He's setting down roots.

Raym had asked Lah and me not to come, wanted to protect our cherished memories of Mackie. He didn't want us to see the savage toll of colon cancer on her body. Raym believed that the vibrant woman we remembered, full of laughter and life, was far better preserved in our minds than replaced with the fragile shadow that remained. Though she'd undergone several difficult surgeries and compliantly endured the recommended courses of harsh chemotherapy and radiation, they'd stopped all treatments about two months ago, finally accepting that it was futile.

Even the oncologist had acknowledged that there was more misery than benefit. A palliative care team had been introduced, and, with pain management only, the past couple weeks had been a brutally slow process of organs shutting down one by one. There seemed to be no end to the suffering, and visitors were now limited as Mackie was in and out of consciousness.

Lah and I were prepared for what we would see in that room. We'd talked about it all the way to Louisiana.

I mean, ideally, one would like one's entire life's route to be all coasting as if riding a bicycle down a hill with feet lifted high to enjoy the speed and the breeze, but it's not like that. There are *hitches* that start and stop the fluidity of time. Life is experienced progressively. In pieces. And, if anything, the two of us had been brought up in such a way that we were uniquely poised to have a strong disposition regarding the hitches that were hard— even death.

So we went straight to her, ignoring her depleted state, and I cupped her untethered hand between my own. Lah took it all in for a moment before sitting down on the foot of the bed, thoughtfully rubbing the still legs and feet beneath the covers.

Mackie didn't rouse at first. It didn't appear that she'd heard Raym's announcement that we were there. Her breathing was steady, but shallow like a raspy whisper. Based on the overview he'd given us of her condition, I hadn't expected her to respond, but in the reality of actually being there with her, a weight of unspoken sorrow hovered in the room.

Thinking I would settle in close to her, I looked around to drag a chair over , but just as I started to move, abruptly, she took a long slow breath, squinching her nose up at the same time. If it wasn't for the preacher chaperoning over her, I'd have thought she was about to cut up—it was the same squinched nose from my early teenage years when she'd slyly pointed to the little peters she'd drawn on the back of the church bulletin during Sunday service, her infectious giggles bubbling over uncontrollably.

I gripped her hand harder, smirking at the quick remembrance of that. Oh how we'd giggled at the thought of the deacons walking through the church to clean up any remaining items on the pews. We'd intentionally left our artwork, a harmless act of rebellion in the sanctity of those hallowed walls.

A slight cough nearby snapped me back to the present, a reminder that I hadn't acknowledged the preacher's presence. I looked up and made eye contact with him, and he sprang to life, as if my gaze had been the cue he'd been waiting for. It felt as if he'd been holding his breath, waiting on Lah and me to arrive so that he could get on with things. His posture straightened, signaling that his moment had arrived.

"Could we all pray?" he asked softly, tilting his head and raising his eyebrows a bit. Then he closed his eyes tightly and began before anyone could reply.

Lord, I thank you for this precious saint.

His voice was suddenly much stronger and authoritative.

I know, Lord, that she's been in your hands all along. And Lord, we don't know why she's had to endure this trial, but we trust you. We trust you, Lord, for every breath we take and we know that you have a purpose and a plan. And now, Lord, we ask you to heal her body. We ask you to touch her from every hair on her head to the soles of her feet. And we will always give you the praise. We ask this in the mighty name of Jesus, the name above all names. Forever and ever. Amen. And amen.

We'd instinctively joined hands as he prayed: Raym and Bingo on the far side of the bed and Lah still next to me. Lah slowly released Bingo's right hand and my left, returning her focus to the legs beneath the covers. She worked indiscriminately, moving back and forth between squeezing each foot and lightly massaging Mackie's calves, her touch tender and gentle.

It was a precious, lingering moment, thick with the deep love that only comes from years of shared memories and unspoken understanding, and I felt Mackie's frail fingers tighten around my hand, so I leaned in.

With a slight, devious grin, she whispered, "He just prayed for my wig that's in the closet." She'd long been bald from the chemo and was wearing a soft beanie to keep her head warm.

She didn't open her eyes.

Suddenly, seeing that the mischievous antics were still alive inside a body that was worn out, the thought of losing her was so heavy and bitter that I burst into tears. It was a ragged and uncontrolled cough cry that startled us all.

The hand that I held immediately pulled away and slapped the bed as if to get our attention.

"Dry it up!" Mackie scolded, hoarsely, and louder than expected. I was still looking at her wide-eyed when she spoke again.

"I'm not scared," she said, firmly. Her voice, though strained, was infused with the stubborn strength that reminded me of the countless times she'd faced challenges head-on through the years. Even in a depleted state, the spirit of the woman I adored still burned bright, refusing to be extinguished by fear.

The room became quiet for a long moment. The kind of deafening silence where trivial sounds like a stomach gurgling or loose change jingling in a pocket become overbearing. A line from a well-known Emily Dickinson poem absurdly flashed through my mind: *I heard a fly buzz—when I died.* The realization dawned that *she knew* just how close death was and that I needed to say something meaningful to her. It might be my last chance.

Maybe I was the only one who felt it, but there was an uncertainty in the air. Even the preacher seemed unsettled at the way she had defiantly bowed up at death. He was shifting his weight from one foot to the other. The motion made him seem impatient.

"We're still believing the Lord for your healing, Sister Mackie," he said finally, and patted her several times on her right shoulder.

I despised him then. I caught myself as I started to roll my eyes. There is nothing worse than being placated. I am not a fool.

The quiet settled in again, with everyone looking around, unsure what to do. Bingo motioned to us in a charade-like way and mouthed that she was stepping out to call the palliative care team back.

"You think y'all could sing?" Mackie eventually asked, her voice wasn't as strong as before.

"*I don't sing*, Mackie, you know that, but I bet Raym and Lah . . ."

"Sing," she cut me off.

I was still wiping my nose with the back of my hand, completely exasperated. I am always more afraid of regret than failure, so I hated not having a plan for the moment.

I looked at Lah, questioningly, who lifted her hands and shoulders into the air in a shrug before getting an idea. Walking over to the small wardrobe, Lah pulled out Mackie's suitcase. Knowing exactly what she was looking for, she unzipped the large compartment on the cover and smiled broadly as she retrieved a tambourine.

"Yes!" Lah said victoriously, shaking the tambourine into the air so that the jingles sounded loudly before beginning to bump it against her other hand in a slow, steady beat.

We all knew Mackie's long-standing rule of carrying a tambourine "just in case."

The out-of-place sound echoed in the room, cutting through the silence. Energized, Raym jumped into gear, softly clapping to the same beat.

"Hmmmm . . ." Raym hummed an extended note to get a key going, and Lah found the note with him. It was obvious he wasn't sure yet what they were going to sing. I joined in the clapping, making eyes at them both that asked if they had a plan.

Finally, Raym snapped his fingers to the beat a few times and began to sing, getting a running start as if he'd caught the song mid-way.

> *Well . . . I wouldn't take nothing for my*
> *journey now.*
> *I'm gonna make it to heaven somehow.*
> *Though the devil tempts me and tries*
> *to turn me around . . .*

Eyes still closed, Mackie started tapping the bed to the beat, and I nudged Lah, directing her attention to it.

Lah nodded and pressed the tambourine under Mackie's fingers, helping her lift her hand a few times with it. There was nothing Mackie liked better than an old Pentecostal hymn, and, realizing that she was now carrying the music for the performance, she became excited.

She started trying to bump the tambourine in 4/4 time, hitting every beat and quickening the pace.

Raym's face twisted as he watched her. Tears were dripping from his cheeks unchecked, but he pressed on, leading the song that he, Lah, and now Bingo were singing. His voice was a steady anchor, providing a measure of comfort and strength amidst the emotional tide that threatened to overwhelm us all.

He's offered everything that's got a name.
All the wealth I want and worldly fame.
If I could still I wouldn't take nothin'
for my journey now.

In a sudden surge, Mackie's arms started windmilling, flailing. It was taking all the strength she had, but she didn't stop. She began saying something repeatedly, or perhaps singing, though there was no audible sound. Even with the encumbrances of the IV on the back of her hand and the pulse-ox on her right pointer finger, she continued waving both arms.

On a table in the corner of the room, I spotted a floral arrangement and a plush stuffed dog beside it. Barry the Basset Hound was printed on the exaggerated tag hanging from its collar. Grabbing the toy, I nestled it in the crook of Mackie's cheek and neck.

The ethereal is a bright light to walk toward, but it is also a soft caress to provide comfort on the journey. If it weren't for Mackie, I would not have known this. I would not have stepped forward—I'm not talking about this hospital room, mind you.

Mackie and her insistence on the softness of death taught me to trust, though it took me the entirety of my youth to do so, and though it didn't mean anyone else would trust in the same, unique way.

The singing had gradually become louder. A concerned nurse popped her head into the room, and, seeing all the commotion, thought Mackie was struggling, that she was reaching out for help and needed something for the pain. She rushed to her side to try to constrain her, hold her arms down.

Mackie had signed a Do Not Resuscitate order. We were all aware.

"Leave her alone!" I screamed, vehemently.

That tambourine, that stuffed toy, the accordion that was surely in the trunk of her car, the little puppies she taught me about from a young age, and even the little peters. I knew that all love stories stemmed from the one I was witnessing in that hospital room.

All love flows outward to be given away.

The MOIALT acronym that I'd been fascinated with came alive to me while I watched Aunt Mackie dying. MOIALT had been inscribed on the double headstone for more than 10 years now—ever since Uncle had died from a heart attack and the loving cameo of he and Mackie in their younger days had been centered above the letters in a domed glass. It had been etched so purposefully, and now its meaning seemed to hum softly around us, as though it had been waiting for this moment all along.

MOIALT. My Once In a Lifetime.

While it appeared Mackie was worshipping to the old hymn instinctively—perhaps from muscle memory of leading a congregation—from my vantage point I saw that she was actually reaching for her beloved.

And I had the unexpected realization that MOIALT referred to a love much bigger than Uncle's. Though their story was sweet, the typical high school sweethearts who only ever dated each other type of story, MOIALT referred more to an eternal love.

Mackie was reaching for Jesus.

The preacher, who had not joined in our singing, backed away. He was startled by all the exuberance, and, of course, by my strong admonishment to the nurse. I saw his bewildered face, gnarled like a stomped insect and now blurred to me through my tears, momentarily arrested as he tried to summon the Christian thing to do.

A doctor in blue scrubs beneath a long white coat came into the room. He was an older sage type with salt and pepper hair and distinguished glasses perched delicately on the bridge of his nose. Walking over to address the alarms now sounding from the monitors at the head of the bed, he silenced them with practiced ease and stepped back, fig-leafing his hands in quiet respect. He perceptively realized the circumstances he'd stepped into, an unspoken acknowledgement of the gravity of the moment.

Studying each of us closely, he offered the kindest smile I think I've ever seen. It was a smile that validated the shared human experience, even when difficult. I surmised that he must be a mentor or shepherd to a flock of young doctors who depended on him to teach them the way. He had a quiet strength about him, the kind that filled the room without a single word.

His reassuring presence spurred me on.

Resolutely walking around the bed, I stepped in front of the preacher, displacing him, moving as close as possible to Mackie to sing into her ear. As I edged closer, I could feel her shallow breaths, each one more fragile than the last.

Setting aside my annoyance at the uncomfortable nurse with her mouth still agape as well as the inhibition of my own off-key voice, I allowed that assuring smile to hold me as I finally joined in the refrain:

> *He's offered everything that's got a name.*
> *All the wealth I want and worldly fame.*
> *If I could still I wouldn't take nothin'*
> *for my journey now.*

I'm not sure how many times we repeated it.

I was caught in a hitch of "no time"—rubbing that stuffed dog against her cheek, belting out the hosanna like a trumpeter leading a glorious processional, and thinking about how I'd sure love to have a ragtag little band like us surrounding me when I die.

I was still fixated on that kind smile when the great physician eventually nodded at us all again and made to step out of the room. He was aware more so than I that his part was done; a transition had occurred.

The tambourine was still.

. . . what is that you express in your eyes?
It seems to me more than all the print I have read
   in my life.

—Walt Whitman, from *Song of Myself*

NINE

Secession

(1997)

Once, when I was a teenager, we had driven over to bring some fresh butter beans to Ms. Donnie who lived at the top of a long, private lane off the Lena-Flatwoods Road, when, as we stood at her front door, we heard the hollow, roaring *auuwww* of a big truck drawing near.

Ms. Donnie had a brick ranch-style house, but it still had the traditional Southern front porch, accessed by three steps. The house faced Ms. Ella Mae's and Ms. Watkins' (Ms. Ella Mae's mother), who lived next door to each other on the opposite side of the road, though their houses were the old wood-frame style and not set as far back. In fact, Ms. Watkins' house was older than she was, and she would turn 101 that year. We visited each of these three regularly, sharing items from our garden that typically stank and that I wouldn't eat.

Butter beans always reminded me of the silver-gray bodies of blood-inflated ticks.

I don't know why I noticed it that day—that despite Ms. Donnie's house being brick, which wasn't common then, it still featured the traditional stairs and porch almost mandated by the invisible rules of living in the rural South. It was one of those moments when, though you've seen something over and over again, out of nowhere, you realize you'd never really seen it correctly. Anyway, while we were standing on the porch at Ms. Donnie's, that truck caught the attention of her beloved hound dog, Boon.

He was sprawled lazily by the door and, instantly, his head jerked up, then his entire body started bouncing with excited barking. He sprang to life in an all-out blind run and *roh roh roh roh roh,* with the gait of a cheetah.

We turned to watch the truck pass, knowing from many similar attempts that the dog could never catch it and that the chasing was just for sport . . . only to see him run so fast that one of his long ears, flying forward with the force of his running, grazed a back wheel, which pulled him up and over in a circular arc. We saw him slammed violently against the highway twice with the turns of the tire, his body already stiff, before being flung by the momentum into the ditch.

Ms. Donnie had opened her front door for us just in time to see it too. She immediately knew Boon was dead, but only hesitated a moment with the door ajar before she refocused, and, sweeping her arm into the house in welcome, said graciously, "Why don't you two come on in? I'll get us some iced tea."

The truck never slowed.

Bingo and I sat in the living room, and I looked through the glass storm door out into Ms. Donnie's front yard and toward the road.

I wondered exactly where Boon had landed, and if she would go get him to give him a proper burial.

But not a word was said about it.

Bingo immediately started talking about the most recent "Crown of Thorns" quilt she and Ms. Donnie had been working on with the Eastern Star ladies, even though she had to speak loudly as Ms. Donnie was in the kitchen.

The "Crown of Thorns" pattern was comprised of carefully arranged triangles in three distinct colors and varying sizes, arranged so that the outer row formed a crown-like ring meant to represent the crown placed on Jesus' head when He was crucified.

It had taken years for the group to master the complex design, and now they had so many requests for them they'd never get to them all. Even with the adept quilters seated elbow to elbow around the form every Tuesday morning in the all-purpose room at the church, it took months to complete a single hand-sewn quilt.

The church ladies would work until noon, returning every Wednesday for choir practice followed by prayer meeting, and then report again on Sunday where they'd move through the planned song set according to what they'd practiced mid-week.

"My favorite was the one we finished last fall," Bingo said, admitting that she wasn't fond of the color scheme of the current quilt project.

"That one last fall kind of reminded me of royalty," she continued.

"Oh, *that was* the best," Ms. Donnie said, distractedly emphasizing her agreement.

From where I sat, I could see her side profile and noticed her hands shake as she put ice into the glasses, twisting and cracking the plastic trays to loosen the square blocks, large enough to almost see through, even with their fractures and tiny shattered crystals creating suspended gray spaces. When she turned her back to us to face the sink and fill the trays with water again, I saw her shoulders sag. She wiped tears with a dish towel when she thought we weren't looking, trying to hide her grief.

"What were the names of the three rich shades we used for that one?" Bingo called out, trying to keep the quilting conversation going. "Violet, periwinkle . . . and . . . *what was the last one called, Donnie?*"

Ms. Donnie didn't appear to hear her. She came into the living room and placed a tray of iced tea and cookies on the coffee table, next to a bowl of shiny plastic fruit. Moving the basket of butter beans from her favorite chair, she settled into it, across from where we sat on a tweed couch, its cushions protected by a clear vinyl overlay.

"It's alright," Ms. Donnie finally said, her voice soft, but distant.

I couldn't tell if she was talking to us or to herself, maybe finishing a conversation we hadn't heard. Her words felt suspended, like they'd been waiting for the right opportunity to surface.

A few moments passed, and I could feel Bingo growing restless beside me, trying to figure out how to bring the conversation and Ms. Donnie back to the topic of their quilt-making.

But Ms. Donnie wasn't in that living room with us anymore. Her eyes had gone glassy, looking past us as if she was seeing something we couldn't.

Slowly, she turned and looked right at me, a faint smile on her lips, but it wasn't the kind of smile that brought comfort.

Leaning forward, she grabbed both of my hands, squeezing them tightly.

"You know, Missy," she said, her voice suddenly steady, "in the end, these things we hold on to so tight don't matter like we think they do. They really don't."

My heart was beating in my ears. I wanted to understand what she was seeing, why she was suddenly so sure. Her smile was offering some hidden truth, but I couldn't find it. I strained, trying to reach beyond the veil of understanding that separated us, but it was like looking through fog.

The harder I tried to grasp her meaning, the further away it seemed.

"Missy . . . it's OK," Ms. Donnie finally said, her voice softening as she saw my struggle.

"You and your mama—there's always gonna be a line between you two. It's like the way we were raised, how the world taught us to see things narrow from the time we were little girls."

At that, Bingo fidgeted beside me, the vinyl crackling beneath her. She looked uncomfortable, like she wasn't sure whether to agree with Ms. Donnie or run from whatever it was she'd just glimpsed. Her face was tight, unreadable, as though she'd stumbled onto something she hadn't known was there and now wasn't sure she wanted to keep. Her eyes darted nervously, betraying the unease she tried to mask, and for a moment, it seemed as if the weight of the unseen truth was pressing in on her from all sides.

She had the frustrated look of being off balance.

Suddenly, Ms. Donnie couldn't help it anymore and went running outside toward the ditch.

I was still staring after her when I felt my arm being jerked. We left our glasses of iced tea untouched and hurriedly walked to the car to head home without a sideways glance at Ms. Donnie.

Out of the corner of my eye, I saw her sitting near the road, legs outstretched, head in her hands. She was wearing a dressing gown and her hair was in rollers beneath a handkerchief. Though she was a widow, in that moment I envisioned her as a young bride making herself ready for her wedding.

Boon's head was cradled in her lap.

Over a decade later, I was strangely reminded of this incident. I had returned to Louisiana and was nearing the end of my first year of teaching at a small, private college. My academic focus had always been journalism, but since I had completed a second major in English, I also taught basic composition courses required for most degrees.

To culminate the semester, I had taken my class of freshmen to tour Little Eva Plantation in Cloutierville, Louisiana, twenty-five miles south of Natchitoches. The famed plantation was the inspiration for Harriet Beecher Stowe's 1852 novel, *Uncle Tom's Cabin,* a cornerstone of anti-slavery literature.

Known originally as Hidden Hill, the 11,000-acre plantation was renamed in the 1950s in tribute to Eva, the endearing character from the novel. Eva was a young, white girl whose kindness highlighted the brutal moral divide of slavery. It was a complex dynamic—not just slavery, but economics, and states' rights—all of it boiling over into the Civil War.

I had hoped our field trip would bring these divisive issues into sharper focus for my class, to make them real, not just words on a page. They had just read the novel for their final research paper. It felt like the visit to the plantation was a necessary pilgrimage, one that would help them understand the history behind the narrative we'd been discussing.

But all morning, they had been disengaged with the tour, talking among themselves, the reality of the history somehow not touching them. That is, until our petite tour guide began speaking. She was a cheerleader type—pretty, blonde, and confident, and looked about the same age as my students.

At first glance, I thought her youth and demeanor might encourage them to remain checked out, but her passion caught us off guard.

It was unexpected, almost jarring.

As she explained the daily existence of those who had been enslaved at Hidden Hill, the air in the room seemed to tighten. She described the backbreaking labor in the heat, the violent punishments, and the endless days of living without freedom, sparing no details.

"That was a different time," one of my students abruptly interrupted. He was the most popular in the class—charismatic, always quick to speak up. His tone was almost dismissive, like he couldn't reconcile the dark past with the idyllic setting around him. After all, we were on the grounds of a charming tourist attraction that was fondly known as the largest pecan orchard in North America. Little Eva pralines and quaint Southern keepsakes are shipped around the world.

The guide paused, thoughtful, but didn't waver. "Yes," she said evenly, "but why does that change anything?"

She squinted slightly, tilting her head like she was searching for the right words. "Were those people any less human than we are?"

The question struck a chord. A few girls stopped digging through their purses and looked up. One of the guys slipped his pager back into his pocket.

It was as if they were realizing for the first time—*it happened here. Right here.*

Likening our guide to a modern-day Eva, I made a mental note to thank her later for catching their attention. All semester they'd read each text with detachment, like watching the evening news on television with its stories of devastating war and famine and then flipping the channel unfazed to *Seinfeld* or *Friends*.

Her passion had broken through.

The tour continued, now more somber. We walked beneath rows of pecan trees, their branches casting a dappled light over us. The breeze, the May warmth, felt heavy somehow, as if it carried the burden of the stories we'd just unearthed.

Our next stop was an old clapboard house, a shack really.

"Clementine Hunter was born here," our guide explained. "You might know her name. She's one of the most famous folk artists in Louisiana. She couldn't read or write and came from a family of farm laborers. Her grandmother was a slave."

The shack, now a gift store, was filled with reproductions of Hunter's paintings—crude scenes of plantation life, like picking cotton, tending livestock, or working in vegetable gardens, each one capturing the hardship woven into daily routines. The students recognized the art, but it was as if "Eva" was helping them see it for the first time.

"Her early work sold for just 25 cents," she continued. "Now, her paintings go for thousands."

She paused, noticing the student who had interrupted earlier standing quietly before a vibrant painting of a flowerpot filled with purple zinnias. He reached out and began tracing the outline of the petals with his finger.

"I wonder why she chose *purple*," he said softly, almost to himself, his voice trailing off.

I nearly rolled my eyes, assuming he meant to trivialize it, but then I caught the change in his expression. He was an art student, and he understood the rarity of the color. He knew that purple had long been reserved for royalty or the elite.

His hand, tracing the edge of the flowers, had quieted the group, drawing them in.

It wasn't mockery. It was reverence.

He began explaining to the others how bold it was, back then, to use purple.

And for the first time all day, the class hung on every word. As he spoke, they watched him and our Eva as they stood together at the front of the room, and they suddenly began seeing Clementine Hunter in a completely new light—a bold rebel, defying convention with a single, deliberate choice.

The room fell still. Slowly, one by one, the students began following the path of his finger, their eyes tracing the petals. They weren't just looking at the painting anymore. As they watched the repetitive motion intently, it was as though they could feel something moving within themselves as well. I felt the stirring too.

The reverence in the room was undeniable, and I had one of those moments again—when you see something new in something you've always seen the same way.

In fact, the moment stretched out, and it seemed that the entire room was suffused with a purple glow.

"So very impressive," the student said at last. His voice carried not just admiration for Hunter, but respect for what she represented.

He seemed to grasp, maybe for the first time, that art, history, and the power to shape the world were all within reach. He was giving her a kind of recognition she never would have known in her lifetime.

And just like that, he and our Eva now shared an understanding, their eyes meeting as if acknowledging a silent pact. The pair understood the moment for what it was—that rare instance when all were one, entranced, with the same light in their eyes. The students, who'd started the day distracted, by their own volition were brought into new enlightenment, that fleeting thing.

I knew then that they were all looking beyond those purple zinnias. They had their eyes fixed on something in the distance, began to run toward it. Like watching Ms. Donnie years ago, I felt them gathering their courage and knew I was witnessing another revolution.

Stop this day and night with me and you shall
      possess the origin of all poems . . .
You shall no longer take things at second or third
      hand, nor look through the eyes of the dead,
      nor feed on the spectres in books.
You shall not look through my eyes either, nor take
      things from me,
You shall listen to all sides and filter them from
      yourself.

—Walt Whitman, from *Song of Myself*

TEN

The Shivaree

(2009)

"Lah was home last weekend… got to hug her neck… whispered in her ear… told her I loved her…"

Raym texts and emails as if he is writing a telegram. With a doctorate in communications, I cringe at his writing style, but I love the story material I find in his truncated notes. Always speaking as if the recipient knows what he's talking about, his seemingly coded messages can be hilarious.

If I call and he doesn't answer, I might get a text that says, "With OTom… under the bean…"

No explanation, just a cryptic clue.

OTom is my Uncle Tommy and "the bean" is the 1960 Chevrolet Impala hardtop Raym and his brother have spent the past two years restoring. While I've loved most of the antique cars that have cycled through the garage over the years, especially the 1946 Dodge and the 1929 Model A, I dislike the style of the Impala with its exaggerated tail fins. I hate the color too, and deemed it "the big, green lima bean," a nickname that took hold.

Raym means that he will call me back later.

All through my years away from Sharp at school, before texting was a thing, Raym wrote emails in this same shorthand format. No one could convince him that a return at the end of a line was unnecessary. He was stuck in manual typewriter mode, complete with two incorrect spaces after every thought. Combine the constant line breaks with his *dot dot dot* style, and his emails were jagged and ran for pages—but they were full of information. With a degree in history, his knowledge was fascinating. Raym knew the importance of details.

Recently, I was watching a television series about a North Korean soldier who protected a South Korean woman when she'd inadvertently found herself in North Korea. He'd risked his life to help her return home.

I texted Raym: *Have North and South Korea always been two different countries?*

His response was almost immediate: *Since 1950... when the communists, in the north... supported by China and Russia... attacked the south... supported by the US after 3 years of war (the Korean War)... they reached an armistice... no peace treaty... technically, they are still at war today... South Korea came to be a modern industrial state... while the north is a communist dictatorship... your Uncle Sonny was there with American forces during the war... the dividing line between the two Koreas is the 38th parallel...*

I stared at the message for a long time and finally told myself I'd come back to it. It was too much to process during commercials.

I truly will come back to it. There's much to be studied. Raym always blends facts, historical context, and personal commentary in such a way that I want to know more. I love to press him to tell stories of the past, stories with depth that often make his infectious laughter ring out—always three jerking head nods and a "*shook shook shook*" sound that most people wouldn't think is laughter at all.

Lah and I have mimicked it for years. OTom too. In fact, six years older than Raym, OTom goes beyond mocking the laugh. He relishes any opportunity to add color to an understated incident by inserting particulars that Raym has purposely left out, usually some peculiar trait or quirky habit of Raym himself.

"Aww Raymond," OTom will say, rolling his eyes. "You always leave out the part where *you ran*! You loved to leave Burel and me standing there to take the blame!"

As he talks, he's pantomiming Raym's "chicken run," which wasn't named for his cowardice, but for its spastic style—a gangly flailing of long legs combined with a rigid, immovable backward arm stance that forces his head forward. Everyone knows Raym's run.

"This is the view I remember most," OTom will laugh, yelling over his shoulder and showing his back.

The two are in their 70s now, and "cute" is the word all of us grown children use to describe them as they work on one antique car project after another. Their sister, Mackie, and their brother, Burel, died within the past ten years or so—both at 67 years old, so the remaining siblings are closer than ever. They are the remnant and they now *remember* easier than they *know*. They remember and their stories are more real to them than their today. They remember the Fletcher boys and the Paul boys, and the Beebes, the Martins, speaking of them in wistful tones, reliving youthful friendships that still eddy through their hearts, the current alive and flowing.

So when Raym texts that he's with OTom under "the bean," there's 70-plus years of shenanigans—pure, but shenanigans still—that that very car could have rolled through with them.

Or some other hooptie. Maybe a 1940 Ford one ton flatbed truck with the whole band of brothers from the community riding on the back and holding on as best they can. A group of teenagers roaring down Highway 8 doing fifty, fifty-five, peeling out of Castor Lane, heading towards Flatwoods, thinking they'd go faster if the beater they'd scraped up the money for and got running was up for it. The brothers talk of these days with no aspirant dreams, telling stories fully aware that no one past their dwindling generation will appreciate them and remaining perfectly reconciled and content with the state of life *as they remember it.*

Blissfully happy. It's rare. Enviable.

In fact, it seems to me that all the men who grew up in Sharp have been roaring up and down Highway 8 their whole lives, in newer, shinier cars before they knew it, and as they've aged they've clamored more and more for what they now realize was better all along. They tell the stories of those days so convincingly that I've reached the point that, at any moment, I might believe it so myself. Indeed, as one who guides students to deconstruct stories to better understand them, I find myself listening to Raym and OTom, constantly looking backward and unable to stop greedily grasping for the blur of glory of their generation.

Driving to the college for a full day of teaching sophomore English, contemplating a story for the focus of the day's discussion, I smile at Raym's text about seeing Lah, ". . . whispered in her ear... told her I loved her..."

Lah and I have grown up warmed by stories that keep the blur of glory vibrant and alive to us—anecdotes like Burel diving through a church window in a brawl of deacons and Mackie playing "boogie woogie" during a frenzied Pentecostal altar service. We've participated in exploits like the congé. And Lah's relationship with Raym was the impetus of her unique wedding, a story itself.

In 1998, when Lah's fiancé, Ben, finally finished his graduate program in poultry science at the University of Arkansas, Raym helped Lah plan a special evening wedding at the pavilion of Campbell Creek Cemetery. It sounds crazy, of course—a wedding at the cemetery—but the pavilion, blanketed in an infinite sea of miniature white lights, with mounds of airy tulle wisped around its columns and huge bouquets of cut dogwoods and pink roses, was quite a romantic setting. Though on the cemetery grounds, the pavilion is situated adjacent to the actual burial area in such a way that graves would not be in eyesight during the ceremony.

Not that Lah would have minded that.

While most would cringe at seeing a grave during a wedding, Lah spent her nervous hours before the ceremony comfortably pacing from the first double headstone near the entrance gate down the path between the oaks that flank the tiny tombstone of the Martin's stillborn baby and back again, letting her fingers graze the top of every marker as if tousling the hair of those watching. At 5-foot-2, she is just the right height to give a casual, reassuring pat to each—without so much as a bend of the knee. Like me, Lah has always had a unique relationship with the cemetery, seeing it more as a garden.

So using the pavilion was the perfect idea, really, fully appropriate for Lah, and guests went along with it, appreciating the charming venue. It was a beautiful spring evening with a light breeze. Even the Louisiana humidity offered a brief reprieve. I fully believed everything was on track for a traditional Southern wedding. Well, except that we were at the cemetery.

Lah's plans were moving along flawlessly, without a hitch at all, until, when the parents were seated and soft music began to play for the groom and minister to enter, then suddenly cell phones everywhere buzzed in unison with a one-word text: *Shiv!*

Suddenly, with Raym's group text signaling notice, there was a unnatural, startled outcry. A sound one might make if unexpectedly goosed in the side. A man's muffled voice was heard protesting in playful disbelief. The music changed to a loud New Orleans parade style sound, complete with trumpet and trombone. And then, from the back of the pavilion, Raym came up the center aisle pushing Ben on a vintage-design single-wheel wheelbarrow that he'd made himself.

With family and friends playfully catcalling, Ben had no choice but to laugh and submit to it. He was outnumbered anyway since each row of guests, in on the plan from the beginning, had fallen in line behind Raym as he passed, pulling noisemakers out of their pockets. Raym continued pushing the wheelbarrow past all the rows and on outside, where the string of people circled the building several times, dancing free-spiritedly to the music, which invited participation and exuded the joy of the day. The beat of the brass band was infectious.

Raym's new version of an old-fashioned shivaree lasted only ten minutes, just long enough to mark the occasion, similar to the way Twelfth Night revelers formalize a Mardi Gras with an opening parade. Tut, who had driven in from Hattiesburg (he'd never miss Lah's wedding), intervened to help Raym at times because, at a certain point of each lap around the pavilion, Raym could see Lah sticking her head out of the back area where she'd been waiting for the bridal march hidden from view. Seeing her that way, with just her head poking out from behind a door, made it all the more funny, and he couldn't keep the wheelbarrow aright for throwing his head forward in his *"shook shook shook"* laugh.

Ben was soon deposited next to the minister, a little sweaty and his tux rumpled, but in good spirits. Guests returned to their seats, and Raym pushed the empty wheelbarrow back up the aisle, noticing, with a proud grin, that Ben's parents were wide-eyed. They'd purposely been left out of the group text and hadn't joined in the march, quite taken aback by it all. Even with the event underway, they were still dubious about the cemetery wedding. The bewildered expressions on their faces said more than words could, a mixture of disbelief and cautious amusement.

It took time for Lah to speak to Raym again afterward, but she has a weak place for him, vulnerable, knowing how wonderful it is having someone like him loving her that much, someone always, provenly, good. It's been more than 10 years now, and she remembers it all fondly.

This shivaree, the "new shiv" as we call it in our family, is a story that I could certainly select to deconstruct with my students in the day's class, studying myriad elements as the focal point—Ben's parents' reaction, Raym's elaborate planning, the wheelbarrow he lovingly crafted by hand and hid for weeks, the cemetery setting, and on and on. There are lots of stories within the story.

And here is where I question my deftness as a teacher. Consistently, just as I begin to tell the story, I feel lost. I lose the thread. Even when I try to tell the "story of the shiv" to myself (and I've done so many times), I lose it. Each detail tussles with the next, contending for the lead position, the spotlight; there is no focal point. Though the overall picture is clear in my mind, I find that I center upon a different element each time I begin to tell it. I spew disparate, irretrievable story blocks with no schematic to build anything at all.

But there is one. I'm confounded by it. It's a narrative that originates in the blur of glory that I can see though I'm just slightly too young to fully know.

Raym and OTom's grandmother, Sybil Knight Martin, was a widow, having lost her husband, Kary, in 1935. Her life was marked by resilience as she raised her children alone during a time when such challenges were all too common. Later in life, with four grown children, their "Granny Martin" married Elias Beebe, whose wife, Liddie, had also died. Their connection, born from shared experiences of unexpected loss, seemed almost serendipitous.

The wedding was a simple affair at the courthouse in Alexandria, attended by a few family members and some of their children (there were 10 children and many grandchildren between them). There was no reception afterward or celebration. No fanfare at all. Both self-effacing and pragmatic, the new couple just wanted a simple supper together at home.

On that Friday evening, their sacred honeymoon night, what came to be known as the "old shivaree" occurred. The brotherhood was all there—Buddy Martin; Gus, Jerome, and Jerry Lee Fletcher; RK, Harlis, and Huey Beebe; Rodney Paul; and OTom (known as Tommy then), Burel, and Raym.

Raym, the youngest, was the lookout, peeking from behind one of the massive oaks that flanked the front porch of the shotgun-style wood-frame house while Tommy shimmied through a window that had been left raised a few inches in the August heat. This is where some say that, seeing a partial pone of cornbread left out on the kitchen counter, Tommy stopped and cut himself a thick wedge, soaking it in a glass of cold milk and eating it with a spoon before he eventually crept over to unlock the front door. No one knows for sure, but it took a few minutes before the door was opened, and more than one attests that he was wiping crumbs from his mouth.

The troupe of boys charged in and danced back and forth through the center alley of the house while Granny Martin and Elias, now called Uncle Elias, locked themselves in the bedroom.

The boys howled, banged pots and pans, shook cowbells, scraped washboards, and blasted horns—a discordant cacophony of sound to celebrate the nuptials, albeit in an uninvited way. Their laughter rang out, a joyous yet mischievous soundtrack to the chaos unfolding. The procession then moved outside, tramping around the house as the banging and hollering continued, with the boys now knocking on the window of the bedroom too. In any good shivaree, the groom has to be routed out.

Regrettably, with each boy rapping on the window with a whoop as he went by, one of them, drunk on homemade muscadine wine, hit the window too hard. Being the shortest of the crew, he was reaching up and tapping the window with the metal water dipper he'd grabbed from beside the washbasin near the back door on one of their laps around the house.

The sound of glass breaking and falling was immediately sobering. In mid-step, the boys froze in place, unsure what to do next . . . until they saw the barrel of Uncle Elias' Winchester 12-gauge shotgun coming through the hole in the window.

The mad scramble was epic then. They stumbled over each other as the panic set in.

Burel, who had eased his old pickup close to the house (the plan was to force Uncle Elias into the truck bed to continue the shivaree throughout the community), suddenly became the getaway driver. Grabbing anything they could to hold on, the boys dove headfirst into the bed of the truck from all directions— all but Raym who, again, was the youngest and too slow to catch up.

As Uncle Elias fired a warning shot into the air, Burel gunned the engine into a throaty roar and burned the tires, leaving only a cloud of smoke and the acrid smell of scorched rubber.

With gravel flying wildly, they sped out of the driveway onto Highway 8 seemingly on two wheels, and saw Raym's run as he hightailed it to the nearby bushes to hide.

Raym and OTom are unbeatable when it comes to telling the tale of the old shivaree. And I don't know when I started listening more carefully. I don't know when I broke the chains of my generation, stopped looking off into the distance uninterested, balking, turning a deaf ear, and became more inclined to hear—feeling satisfied with the story.

Somewhere along the way, I lost the trappings of my time. We are all aware of time, always, mind you. What I'm saying is that there are some indelible memories, *if we ingest them,* that heighten our awareness of how fleeting our lives are . . . not to scare us, but to make us cherish every moment.

It's what I see in *the blur* that the wise of my generation long for and try to grasp, and it's what the generation I teach may never take the opportunity to know.

I've been a professor in the Department of English, Journalism, and Languages at Louisiana College for 12 years now. I'm not sure I'll stay here. I'm only 38, and I've already reached the point where, at any given moment, I get caught up in an interim space.

It's a limbo, a moment between what I've known and what lies ahead.

I've tried repeatedly to explain this problem to Lah.

"There's nothing you love better than thinking too much, Missy," she tells me.

"It's what happens when your life revolves around words," I say, envious of her free-spirited nature.

But even though I laugh about it, I'm often flustered trying to teach Tim O'Brien's "The Things They Carried," William Styron's *Sophie's Choice,* and even Kate Chopin's *The Awakening* to indifferent students who wouldn't recognize *the blur* if it were to box them squarely on the nose.

They have no context, no historical basis, no personal commentary, no Uncle Sonny.

"Since 1950... when the communists, in the north... supported by China and Russia... attacked the south... supported by the US after 3 years of war (the Korean War)... they reached an armistice... no peace treaty... technically, they are still at war today..."

How crazy is it that, as an English teacher, I feel as though I'm in a war of my own?

As I begin class, I'm still thinking about Raym's texts and both the old shiv and the new. I finally decide on the story that I will use as the starting point for the day's discussion. I make my choice hopefully, knowing thus far they've not understood the significance of the stories I've shared.

My English 201 students have their desks in a large circle around me.

I stand there recounting the story of the old shivaree, laughing out loud in spurts at my own depiction while stone faces, unaffected and superior, avert their eyes in seeming embarrassment for me. I look from face to face, and, as I turn to study each one, instead of the fun-loving, celebratory processional, it feels as though they are encircling me like a mob.

Describing Raym's fantastic guffaw, I forcefully nod my head trying to model the "*shook shook shook*" that is his alone. I turn in another circle to scan the faces for reaction to that.

And, as our period is nearing the end, I'm jogging around the circle with my elbows pulled back and my chin jutted awkwardly forward in a running style that no one could ever adequately mimic. I up my game, adding theatrics to my performance, attempting to draw them in with my animated gestures and exaggerated expressions.

Perhaps I spend a few more minutes telling the story than I should—knowing the specifics of time and place, the story is very much alive to me. And we are working on descriptive essays this week *for Pete's sake*. I'm telling it thinking that surely my story will help the students look deep within themselves to find a story of their own. I don't deserve the "What does any of this have to do with anything?" that is shot at me.

I slowly turn and look at the student, seeing, as I do so, that the faces of the other students finally show reaction.

I smile. And he smiles. With the rest of the class watching, we have a sort of standoff, looking each other in the eyes with this smile hanging between us.

And I realize . . . he thinks he's showing me compassion. He thinks he's gently teaching me how to be a better teacher.

A boy with a name like *Worth,* who has no appreciation for cars with nicknames like "the bean," a boy who can't fathom choices like the one Sophie had to make, a boy who may never know brotherhood in the way of Tim O'Brien and his Alpha Company and who will probably, you know, leave class, drive through and get a value meal at Burger King or McDonald's before meeting his friends to play Xbox, has just tried to enlighten me.

By the time the three beeps sound to signal the class change, I've made up my mind.

2009 is my last year as a teacher.

Not I, not any one else can travel that road for you,
You must travel it for yourself.

You are also asking me questions and I hear you,
I answer that I cannot answer, you must find out for
  yourself.

—Walt Whitman, from *Song of Myself*

ELEVEN

Showdown at Victory FBC

(2020)

It came in on rollers, with Confederate gray velvet skirting, crisply pleated at the top, attached by Velcro all the way around.

There had just been a procession. A group had been paraded in from somewhere up front (perhaps the room behind the choir loft) to the first four rows on the right side of the sanctuary. Attendants discreetly slipped small pew-back RESERVED tents into their coat pockets as they directed them to their seats.

There appeared to be four generations of family, and I scribbled a note to mention that. Some had tissues in hand; others looked down to carefully place each foot.

A thin elderly man, the last to be seated, came in slowly, reinforced at either elbow by a middle-aged woman. Daughters, I presumed. He was a retired longtime state Attorney General, and my quick research the day before had revealed the couple had three children.

The packed room was still, and the air was growing increasingly heavier with each note of the organ's reverberating "Amazing Grace."

Pipe organs are the worst, I thought, catching myself just as I started to roll my eyes. With a pipe organ, each phrase ebbs and flows, rocks back and forth for emphasis in a way that deepens the sadness, increases the suffering. It's cruel, really.

I uh ONE suh Wah us LOS tuh . . .
Bu ut NOW wah I um FOUND.
Wah us BLIND . . .
bu ut NOW uh . . . I uh SEE.

In this manner, they try to make even the one-syllable words hurt.

When everyone was seated, funeral home attendants began their push from the back as if following some silent prompt. With the size of the family, the decision had been made not to select personal pallbearers (according to the notes in the elegant funeral pamphlet). So, in what seemed to me a double breach of etiquette, the paid escorts wheeled the shiny, gunmetal casket on a cart, slowly rolling it forth as on a caisson.

The attendants were dressed alike and flanked each corner formally, like sentinels. The organist flipped a page in a three-ring binder, and the hymn seamlessly changed to "Precious Lord," a song with a steadier cadence, more fitting for the march.

As soon as they cleared the entryway, a fifth man discreetly closed the double doors behind them and retreated again.

It was very smoothly done indeed, too well I thought, and tried to push away my callousness. I was just settling into the drill when suddenly . . . *eek*!

A sharp sound caught my attention.

Looking around, I was still trying to identify it, when, after a short pause, there it was again . . . *eek*!

With each slow rotation, one of the casket cart's wheels was squeaking, a painfully shrill and discordant noise. I imagined the fifth man looking through one of the single windows on the closed doors and cringing in horror, embarrassment.

I watched the faces of the crowd as, gradually, each one began to identify the sound and then pretend not to hear it. In a way, it lifted some of the weight in the room.

And then, as if the squeaky wheel wasn't enough, I saw them: the tiny clear plastic straps used to keep the funeral spray righted atop the casket. Dozens of beautiful, uniformly poised pink roses were forcibly held in place, manipulated and phony.

I can't believe they did that.

The squeaking ended as the casket was positioned in front of the altar. The attendants stepped back together, facing it in a perfect line to pause for a moment in respect.

Then, perhaps after some silent gesture or planned timing, the two flanking attendants began to systematically arrange the many stands of flowers, bringing some closer, nestling them around and balancing the presentation with care. The rest of the arrangements were used to create a sort of abatis between the minister and the people; they were splayed out left and right across the front of the church. When satisfied, the pair turned and walked together back up the aisle.

The remaining two stepped forward then, one gingerly lifting and holding the front half of the casket's top while the other reached inside and pulled up an unobtrusive bar to keep it propped open. A pleated, white satin overlay apron was positioned, covering the front as if to soften the metal edge.

Satisfied with their display, they made eye contact and together withdrew, revealing in their stead, from my vantage point, the top of a cheek and a nose.

The execution was flawless. Across the front of the church, each of the oversized, standing flower sprays was fortified at its base with more modest potted plants. There were no gaps. It was such an impressive array.

But I couldn't stop thinking it was a sham. All of it. Though tilted at a 45-degree angle now, those roses remained perfect.

I hate that they did that. I really do.

The minister stepped to the pulpit and began the service with the opening verses of John 14—

> *Let not your heart be troubled;*
> *ye believe in God, believe also in Me.*
> *In My Father's house are many mansions:*
> *if it were not so, I would have told you.*

The familiar words were meant to comfort and reassure. All the scripture readings in the world wouldn't have changed my mind on anything though.

At every service, there was always something disappointing in the reciting of verse.

It felt just like using those plastic straps.

I don't know what I was yearning for, but surely they had something else in their arsenal. Something that didn't fall flat. I always looked for it.

For eleven years, one of my duties as a reporter has been to cover the funerals of prominent community members for the *Tribune*. As I slipped into my usual seat in the back rows of churches, I often found myself feeling like a weary soldier carrying an empty canteen, searching for the well of solace that always seemed just out of reach. Each service blurred into the next.

Next up were several eulogists.

The loving husband spoke of the 62 years he'd been blessed to have with his sweetheart, his voice trembling with emotion as he recounted their shared memories. A frail sister, in barely audible tones, told stories of their childhood in a small, rural community, recalling long summer days filled with laughter and mischief. A longtime neighbor also spoke, mentioning with humor the stray cat whom they shared, and even playfully fought over, in these last lonely empty nest years, reminding everyone present that love extends beyond the human heart.

A soloist stepped forward and sang "I'll Meet You in the Morning," an integral part of any good church funeral.

Purposely allowing a long pause before stepping back to the podium, the minister concluded with encouraging words to the family, reading Isaiah 41:10 and 13.

Fear thou not; for I am with thee;
be not dismayed; for I am thy God.
I will strengthen thee; yea, I will help thee;
yea, I will uphold thee
with the right hand of My righteousness ...
For I, the LORD thy God, will hold thy
right hand, saying unto thee,
Fear not; I will help thee.

Then, he asked the congregation to stand for the benediction.

The organist was in place to begin the hymn for the recessional where, keeping with etiquette, everyone would have one last viewing of the deceased. I had given up on finding it that day, and, as was my practice, planned to slip out when my row was prompted to fall in line to walk forward.

186

I looked down to close my notebook and tuck my pen into my purse. I had captured all that I needed for my story. I knew, actually, that I could pull one of many old published stories and just update some of the details. They were all the same.

But the music didn't start on queue.

I looked up again just in time to see the organist's mouth drop open and followed her eyes to the minister, whose expression had changed.

If I hadn't been in one of the back rows, I would have missed it.

I might not have seen the haggard man with the overgrown beard and long, matted hair. He had entered unchecked through the heavy double doors in the back (*Where was the fifth man?*) and now began to walk up the center aisle.

One of the four sentinels rushed to catch him, touching his elbow in a leading way and whispering in his ear, urging him to sit down. I noticed a few other men in the audience in a state of hesitation, wanting to offer assistance yet unsure if doing so was appropriate.

The minister had already raised a hand.

"Let him come," he said, his voice steady and welcoming, reflecting the nature of the church itself.

The man, who hadn't been deterred anyway, continued onward. He shuffled more than walked.

He had the appearance of an eccentric professor wearing jeans and a ragged corduroy jacket with patches on the elbows.

I had the thought that, if cleaned up, he'd look to be in his mid-40s.

Moving in a surprisingly straight line, he stopped only when reaching the casket, where his dirty fingers gripped its edge, rumpling and soiling the pure white overlay.

He studied the face within for a long moment, as if trying to memorize every detail.

And slowly—in the stillness of no-time and without musical notes of accompaniment—he bent forward to lovingly kiss that exposed cheek.

The wail, then, was loud and guttural, building from a moan into the sound of an animal, caged too long, that suddenly flails against its imprisoning bars in a crazed spurt of strength and gradually surrenders to its fate, knowing that it only hurts itself.

The man turned toward the source of the cry, the crowd also realizing that it came from the esteemed Attorney General, the family's patriarch, a casualty now crumpled on the front row being consoled by his daughters.

The stone silence in the room intensified, even without the organ.

And if the man knew them, he didn't show it.

He turned back toward the casket, toward the altar, and with one soft press on the chest of his beloved, followed the wall of flowers across the front of the church to exit through a side door, leaving behind a lingering sense of grief that hung heavy above the crowd.

A total stranger leaned over to me and whispered: *That's their youngest child. He's been a Lost Cause for years. But I guess even a drunk has enough respect to say goodbye to his mama.*

I grabbed my notebook.

I knew then that I'd found it. They'd ended the siege with that single cannon shot.

Because nothing was supposed to hurt the way that kiss hurt. It rent through everything, caught us all like an ambush.

Suddenly, I felt victorious, like I'd just won a hard-fought battle. The pain overcame the fact that those roses didn't slide off. It turned that squeaky wheel into the august vehicle of liberty. It did it all really.

It sustained me. It changed my life forever.

I just know it did.

Sure as the most certain sure, plumb in the uprights,
  well intertied, braced in the beams,
Stout as a horse, affectionate, haughty, electrical,
I and this mystery here we stand.

—Walt Whitman, from *Song of Myself*

TWELVE

Fierce Like an Oak Tree

(2023)

There were five bananas in the wicker fruit basket on the kitchen counter. I don't especially like bananas, but I do appreciate their texture over other fruits. Actually, my favorite thing about bananas is that they add order to my day. Unlike grapes, which are bought in bunches and typically not consumed all at once, I can grab a banana as I head out the door and tick a box. *Tick.* My daily fruit intake is done.

Of course, bananas must be eaten at just the right time. Like avocados, there's an invisible countdown clock to the perfect state of ripeness, and when the clock winds down to zero, ready or not, it's time to eat a banana. On Sundays, when I do my grocery shopping, I also enjoy the game of buying the appropriately-sized bunch for the planned week ahead. When the timer sounds and I can start pulling one each day, there's great satisfaction in knowing that I've expertly selected, and I'm not left hanging with more days that week than I have edible bananas. It's just something I hear in my head, but it's there, nonetheless. *Tick.*

There's nothing worse than a brown banana.

I am a corporate writer now. I'm no longer teaching because the language skills of college students who've grown up texting are beyond hope. Their interpersonal skills often seem non-existent as well, making the effort to guide them feel like an unachievable task. Most recently, I worked as a reporter, but I gradually became too jaded to continue—every assignment began to feel the same.

I'd love to be writing stories of my own.

Ironically, however, I've never been successful at telling my own story. For one thing, I get too plain with it. I can sit for hours writing and rewriting a story on the screen, only to delete my work out of frustration. More than anything, I know that there's nothing unique about me to tell. There are things more important than my percipience.

So it's a good fit for me to serve as senior editor for a global mission-focused organization. In this position, I can help amplify the voices of those whose narratives deserve to be heard, allowing me to engage with the complexities of storytelling from a different perspective. My role is to write speeches for our CEO and craft narratives used in videos and social media posts to engage volunteers, encourage corporate donors, and explain the scope of our work—which is to save the lives of people in impoverished nations by providing surgeries they wouldn't have access to otherwise.

I especially like that our work is tangible. It can be counted. A surgery performed. A life saved. *Tick.*

That Monday morning, when my sister-in-law calls, I am working from home and already in my first meeting.

Our department is spread around the globe, and most of my meetings are early to accommodate European and African time zones. I've grown accustomed to this schedule, and I like Teams meetings because I can turn on my avatar and always look shiny and polished.

In fact, 18 months ago, while I was going through chemotherapy, I had my avatar on for the duration of a long all-staff meeting because I was using my fingers to softly lift tufts of hair away from my scalp. I'd been fascinated by how easily a single handful had pulled away, so I just kept going. I made stacks on my desk—at times pressing the piles and watching them spring back. I moved a few wisps to other piles, just to keep them even, almost as if I were arranging pieces of a delicate puzzle, each strand a reminder of a moment I couldn't quite grasp.

While the Chief People Officer was wrapping up the extended call with encouragement to plan for the future by contributing as much as possible to the 401(k) plan and receive the full company match toward retirement, I was running my hands all over my scalp to ensure that I'd efficiently gotten it all. I'd been so proud of myself that, thanks to the avatar, I'd smiled the entire time. Texas Oncology had prepared me well that losing my hair would be part of the standard process, so it was expected. Smooth bald head. *Tick.*

I'm not making light of it though. Cancer is a bitch.

Anyway, it is Monday morning and, as I said, I am in a meeting, so I absent-mindedly click the left side button on my phone to decline the call, making a mental note to reach out to my sister-in-law later. I glance at the clock, thinking the meeting has drifted to topics that don't pertain to my current assignments.

Checking myself in the small inset screen layered above the other faces encapsulated there in perfect rows, equally spaced, I mute myself and turn on my avatar for a brief moment, thinking that I can walk to the kitchen to grab my banana. It's still a bit too early for my second cup of coffee. That's at 10 a.m.

I am just about to step away from my desk when the phone sounds again. Not a call this time, but a text.

CALL ME BACK IMMEDIATELY!!

I don't remember much of the morning after that.

My sister-in-law calmly tells me to pack a bag and travel back home from Texas, where I now live. Raym is in ICU. He'd had a serious heart attack in the wee hours of the morning. It is a "widowmaker," she explains. (She is a nurse, so she knows.)

Then, as I start to ask questions, there is a scuffle. I can tell she is suddenly surrounded by people.

There are muffled voices and . . .

"We just lost him," she says bluntly.

I don't know how she could've made the news hurt any less. Simple, honest, and direct is always best. I work with words. It's common advice I give to others.

But standing in my closet, holding my zebra print travel bag embroidered with *Missy* on the side that I'd jerked off the shelf only moments before, I howl a grief-wail that I've only heard one other time when I covered the funeral of the wife of a prominent lawyer in town.

Near the end of the refined service, the couple's prodigal son had walked in unexpectedly. He'd returned to say goodbye to his mother.

That father's heart ripped as it could not contain the agony. It was unimaginable for the son to finally return *then*. It was too late.

I'd periodically thought about that sound ever since, feeling like an imposter because I didn't think I could write convincingly about something I'd never felt myself. You have to know things before you have the right to say things.

When I realize I am making that very sound, I suddenly think I'm going to vomit.

My sister-in-law continues talking, carefully breaking down every detail of what happened to Raym that morning and what had been done for him . . . not because it matters, but because it reprieves.

I imagine her there in a frenzied hallway outside the ICU surrounded by the shock and chaos of our family's grief while I stand ridiculously in my oversized closet with its floor-to-ceiling racks of clothes meticulously arranged by season and then by color. The contrast feels absurd. Ever since I've begun writing, I've measured the character of those around me, obsessing over their every word and action, and her unwavering bravery in the situation impresses me, making me acutely aware of the strength I need to summon in myself.

"I'll call you back," I finally choke out, and hang up.

The phone immediately sounds again.

It is a text reminder of a doctor's appointment at 2 p.m. At my checkup a few days before, just six months after I'd been given the all clear, my oncologist had frowned after finding something hard near the top of my man-made right breast.

"Probably just scar tissue," he'd said, after squeezing and pressing from all angles. "Let's schedule a sonogram and be sure."

So I respond "Y" to confirm my appointment, all the while thinking how that autogenerated text is like rock salt being viciously scraped through an open wound. I mean, for goodness' sake, *my dad just died and now my cancer might be back*?

Who could imagine a worse day?

"I can't head out until this afternoon," I text my sister-in-law and make myself focus on packing. I take a deep breath, trying to steady the whirlwind of thoughts swirling in my mind, and move to stand in front of the section of dark pants beneath the dark, dressy tops.

I need to regain a sense of order before it slips away again, and the arrangement of clothes in the closet calms me, offering a small measure of peace.

"It's OK, honey," she texts back. "Be careful on the road. We'll see you tonight."

I am a few minutes late for my appointment at Ross Breast Center because I'd spent time in the parking garage powdering my red nose again and again and pressing my tongue against the roof of my mouth to try to regulate my breathing (a trick I'd found by googling "ways to stop crying").

I hurriedly step off the elevator at the sixth floor, open the heavy doors to the waiting room, and turn right to check in at the registration desk—only to run straight into Peggy Newburn from church, who is checking in as well.

We are the last two in a short line.

There's one thing I can tell you for sure about cancer. Everybody knows when you've got it.

So, with a concerned smile, Peggy gives me an extended hug.

"How *are* you?" she asks as she squeezes me, and I can't help but notice the frigid temperature of the room, making the sterile environment feel oppressive.

Her drawn-out tone triggers the interest of a pretty, 40-ish looking woman with long blonde hair sitting close by in the waiting room.

The woman looks up at us and then politely back to her magazine, but I can tell she is listening. Her body language makes me think she might be at the beginning of the process—the multitude of women with breast cancer is so vast that each test, treatment, or surgery is masterfully performed according to a schedule, a kind of grim ballet that unfolds in waiting rooms like this one.

"*Everything is fine,*" I tell Peggy, using a tone that lets her know I've understood her true question. I am consciously speaking in a voice louder than my own to reassure the woman reading the magazine.

"I'm just here for a follow-up," I say, casually. "It's part of the plan."

It wasn't a lie. So far there had been five months of chemo and six surgeries, including a double mastectomy and, after a nasty staph infection, a hard-to-believe procedure where part of my shoulder muscle was slid under my arm without detaching blood vessels to create a new breast.

Then, there had been 33 rounds of radiation and 14 rounds of adjuvant chemo.

There had also been the small box stuck to my belly to deliver additional treatment at home, beeping insistently, when empty, with the same sound the garbage truck makes when it turns around in front of my house on Tuesdays and Fridays.

It had all been planned.

"Oh, I'm so glad," Peggy says. "You've shown such amazing strength and had the best attitude throughout all of this. You've just been an inspiration."

I look away modestly, not sure what to say and feeling awkward, knowing the blonde woman nearby is still listening.

We sit down to wait.

"How's your mama and them?" Peggy asks in the way Southern folks do. "Everyone OK?"

"I'm heading home this afternoon," I say. My cell phone is vibrating away, so I move my purse from my lap to the floor beside my feet.

I'm still chatting with Peggy about her daughter, who happens to share the same birthday as me, when I am called back by the nurse.

Prior to having a double mastectomy, I had biopsies on four different masses.

While two were simple needle aspirations and one was a sonogram-guided core needle aspiration—both very routine and quick procedures—the fourth was a barbaric stereotactic biopsy as the mass was difficult to pinpoint. After the procedure, I had to lie face down with my breast compressed in a sort of lateral mammography machine for an extended time to apply pressure and help stop some persistent bleeding at the biopsy site. The wound was small, but worrisome.

Dr. Leete, the kind radiologist who'd performed all of the biopsies, kept coming in and out of the room to check on me then, knowing it was painful.

While I squeezed my eyes tightly closed and took shallow breaths, he'd counted down the time, asking about my weekend plans and making silly jokes.

So, of course, he remembers me and is surprised to see me again.

"Back for more torture, are we?" he says, laughing as he walks over to study the sonogram images the radiology technician has just displayed on the screen.

"Nothing can hurt me now," I say. "I have no feeling from the inside of my elbow up through my armpit and across my chest. Take your best shot."

Dr. Leete is still grinning as he accepts the sonogram wand from the nurse and rolls it back and forth over the suspicious area himself.

"Sorry the gel is cold," he says.

"What gel?" I snark back, reminding him again that I can't feel anything, although I know from experience that he is making a sticky mess.

After a few more passes, he leans back in his chair. The nurse hands me a towel to wipe the gel, gently touching my wrist and lowering my arm from over my head.

"I don't want to put you through another needle biopsy, and I do want you to have an answer before you leave today," he finally says. "Let's work you into the line for mammography and see if we get confirmation that it's scar tissue from that. We'll go from there."

For the next forty minutes, I am in the secondary lobby where women await their turn for a mammogram wearing a one-size-fits-all pink cape. They put their belongings in a personal locker and are given a key on a stretchy bracelet. Also pink. I have loved the color pink since I was a little girl, but the lowest day of my life was being wheeled out of the hospital thirty pounds heavier with steroid weight, bald, and wearing a Velcro-front pink shirt over four long drain tubes that were stitched in near the top of my ribcage.

I remember having the ridiculous thought that I wasn't wearing any makeup.

After the first few knowing looks from those in the hallways, that damn pink shirt giving it away, I'd kept my eyes trained on the floor all the way to the car.

And my eyes are trained on the floor again in the waiting area. My phone had continued to buzz incessantly, so I'd foolishly peeked at some of the texts. They affect me like a warm hug, bringing my raw emotions to the surface.

When it is finally my turn, the technician positions and presses me into the awkward stance, struggling with the immobility of a firm gel implant beneath recently radiated, tight skin. Radiation makes skin contract unnaturally.

"I'm sorry," she says, as she tugs at me, using more strength to move me into the right position. "This is the most painful mammogram because the implant has to be forced out of the way."

"I'm so sorry," she keeps repeating, though I have been silent, and I realize she is saying this because tears are rolling down my cheeks.

Finally satisfied with my posture, she twists a knob that makes the clear plates tighten further, and she moves to her computer quickly, saying, "Hold your breath."

"Yes!" she smiles. "Got it! This one's good!" The plates immediately retract. Patting my shoulder reassuringly, she hands me a tissue.

"I know that was painful, but it's over now," she says.

She leaves the room and returns a few minutes later with a smiling Dr. Leete, and I'm able to make it to my brother's house in time for a late dinner.

Three days later, along with my husband and grown son (I am in my 50s now), I am in the second car of the funeral cortege, and the driver of the hearse slows to a crawl as we pass in front of Raym's house on the way to Campbell Creek Cemetery. I didn't know this was planned.

Staring at the back of that hearse with its oddly-curtained window as it inches along, the gesture of total respect stops time for me.

It is like a formal salute, a true final send-off for a revered general.

It had been a beautiful service, full of music—just the way Raym would've liked it. Lah spoke, walking through so many nostalgic memories that conveyed her special daughter-like relationship to Raym. Her stories made me laugh through my tears.

Tut and his wife were there too. They'd driven in from Mississippi, and their two college-age sons served as pallbearers.

After all the times Raym had driven us out to the cemetery in some antique car or another, usually after stopping at the Sharp Store for an orange push-up, we are now driving Raym there slowly following the gentle curves of Highway 8 that I know so well.

204

In those heartbreaking moments, as the tires of the hearse in front of me make gradual contact with the road in arcs that flatten and lay bare year after year with each turn, I suddenly realize what I am hearing. Like a spoked wheel clicking from a stuck leaf, there it is: *Tick. Tick. Tick. Tick. Tick. Tick. Tick. Tick. Tick. Tick.*

I feel sure that Peggy Newburn told the other church ladies about how she'd run into me at Ross Breast Center, and that she was proud of me for being so well-adjusted after facing down cancer. She may, in fact, have said how impressed she was by my unwavering faith, painting me as a tower of resilience.

But if she only knew my secret!

Oh, how I have learned to manage life. I have it all counted, you see.

I believe in raising back up after whatever life throws my way, but most things raise up like an acorn, slowly pushing through the soil to become a seedling and then a sapling and eventually an oak. Most things don't raise up like Lazarus all in one go. While there is no doubt in my mind that Jesus can still pull off such feats, *even healing cancer and sparing grief,* I've always reminded myself that "there are people starving in the world" (and made other such comparisons of fates), and I've never had the audacity to ask Him.

From an early age, swinging barefoot from my tree in the front yard and seeing those crosses at the cemetery in perfect formation, repeating into infinity . . . to witnessing the trees creating a sanctuary over Little Eva Plantation with their perfect rows, equally spaced, I've counted my life as planned, with my only responsibility being to keep growing toward the light.

I'm thankful to Peggy for being proud of me, and I sure hope that Raym is looking down at me proud too now, but there is nothing extraordinary about me.

There is no story to tell.

Returning home, a reassuring wave washes over me as I walk into the kitchen to see that there are still five edible bananas in the wicker fruit basket.

Afterword

With the help of the real "Missy," my cousin Melissa Beebe Smith, I recently embarked on a mission to try to capture the essence of what remains of the Sharp Community. I spent a Saturday morning with Sadie Jowers, who was 97 at the time of our visit. Her floor-to-ceiling bookcases laden with dusty photo albums and scrapbooks were overwhelming. Still very mentally alert, Sadie, known as the unofficial historian of Sharp, had many stories to tell. I tried to soak up as much oral history as I could, knowing my time with her was limited. She passed away a few months after our visit.

I also spent a Saturday with Lawrence "Buddy" Martin. We went through his photos, and I heard a fabulous tale about him and his buddies skinny dipping in Big Rocky until a group from one of the churches showed up to baptize their new converts there. I would've loved to have included a story specifically focused on the swimming hole, but I didn't have enough heart left to pursue it. In many ways, working through this narrative has been painful, so I'll hold this story close, hoping he has captured it elsewhere. He's a prolific writer in his own right, and I trust it's in good hands.

I'm so grateful to Sadie, Buddy, and others who were willing to talk with me to clarify details about an obscure and seemingly dying community—including Chris and Stephanie Perkins, Larry Knight, Wendy Randall Basco, and Jerry Riggs. Jerry was another who was especially passionate about Sharp and had archived many photos and even land plats. We had plans to go through his photos to identify each person in them and include them for publication. Unfortunately, both Jerry and his wife, Ginger, passed away in the spring of 2024.

Invested in this project too, Melissa sought out someone to tromp through the woods, now fenced off as private hunting land, to find the remnants of the old swimming hole known as Big Rocky. When compared to what is seen in the few photos I could find from the past, the current day state is heartbreaking.

It's telling that Raym himself tried unsuccessfully to find Big Rocky a few years ago, by going up and down the Lena Road looking for the old path. He knew Sharp better than anyone. Interestingly, my search for photos brought to light an argument as to which swimming hole was Big Rocky and which was Little Rocky—both were in the area. It may be that the answer to this lies in one's generation. As the swimming holes have diminished over time, what I knew as *Big* Rocky was probably the smaller of the two in the 1950s and '60s. As I stated in the beginning, only the seeds of the stories are true, so it is my hope that no one fixates upon confirming these facts. The truth is not the point, anyway.

To have closure on this project, I find myself wanting to justify the odd blending of old church hymns and spiritual themes with Walt Whitman's *Song of Myself*. Yet my only explanation is that it indeed reflects my life. I studied literature, which can be elitist at times, and I grew up in a very unpretentious environment (what some would just call "country"). Over time, I've been able to discern that Walt Whitman and the old Pentecostal hymns are actually saying some of the same things about life, human connections, and spirituality.

I've had fun exploring those common elements.

Music was also essential, as I couldn't write about Raym without it playing a key role. Along with antique cars, music was Raym's passion, and I'm grateful his wife, Sharon, recorded a few short video clips of him in his element—moments that I will forever cherish. As shared in the final story, Raym died unexpectedly from a heart attack on January 3, 2023. I regret not capturing all of his stories and knowledge about Sharp while I had the chance.

In the end, this project took a different direction than I had originally envisioned. In essence, I began it too late, so there were very few old timers left to provide the historical depth that I imagined. Nonetheless, I am still proud of putting effort into this work. Regardless of what survives of Sharp today, I have come to realize that I grew up in the midst of legends and that Campbell Creek Cemetery is the place to which we perpetually return. It holds us.

Connected to this indelible place and the community that surrounds it are those whose lives and memories have given me the strength to face any obstacle of life. They have shaped my identity, making me fierce like an oak tree.

There, in the Sharp Community, are the arching, tunneling oaks that have faithfully embraced everything—even me. Their roots run deep, binding the past to the present, uniting the stories of those who came before, and reminding me that I am never alone. It is sublime.

The oaks have witnessed birth, death, every homecoming. They stand as silent guardians of a community's shared history. I feel their strength in my bones, in the very core of who I am. It's a quiet power, but it's one that endures.

These days, whenever I drive Interstate 49 South, take exit 103 toward Flatwoods and, after a few miles, pass the ruins of the Sharp Store, see the aging Sharp United Pentecostal Church, and then the old house with the barn-shaped roof set back off the road . . . as I go through the tunnel of trees and then, after curving left, then right, dip sharply left to return to the cemetery once again to bury another one of the greats, my mind has an anointed certainty that is sustained by years of faith and laughter. I am reminded of the deep connections that extend beyond the physical spaces we inhabit.

On that winding, gravel road, I know that I am rooted by a sense of place no matter where I am.

I love that "all of life is a song" (probably an old Pentecostal hymn), and I smile knowing that the song continues with me.

I realize that we cannot see clearly until we can look behind us. Writing these stories has had me looking back more often, and, in the clarity that distance brings, I can see that there is a great invisible chain of destiny pulling each part of our lives into its proper place. When everything is finally in line the way it's supposed to be, things are just . . . well, *right*.

I believe that this chain connects us through generations and on into hallowed places we've yet to experience. I believe that we should never say goodbye because there's no such thing as "was." I believe that our mistakes and prayers and redemptions benefit those who come behind us.

And, finally, I believe that life is worthwhile and fun and—it's just really something.

Surely, you know what I mean.

Story Notes

Light of Mine, though first, was actually the last story written for this project. It provides some historical context about the Sharp Community, situating it within rural central Louisiana, and introduces key landmarks.

The Sharp Store is only mentioned briefly, but it was significant to the community. It's worth noting that, as I talked to different generations, everyone had a "Sharp Store" in mind, though it wasn't necessarily the same store. My grandfather, George Cupples, had two iterations of a general store on Highway 8, next door to his home.

Date unknown. George Cupples' first store in Sharp.

1959. George Cupples in front of his second general store after the first building was relocated. Someone purchased the first building to be used as a home.

Late 1950s. Bill Lyndon Gorum and Raymond Cupples standing in front of Tommy Cupples' 1957 Ford, a car Tommy bought in Nebraska while in the US Air Force.

The store in my memory is neither of these, of course. My generation remembers the Sharp Store that was in the curve on Highway 8 just one-quarter mile from these older locations. All that remains are ruins today. Even the gas pumps are gone.

2024. Remnants of the most recent Sharp Store.

The swimming hole known as Big Rocky sparked much conversation as well, mainly because everyone in the community knows of both a Big Rocky and a Little Rocky. Most Sharp residents consider *Big* Rocky to have been found off the Lena-Flatwoods Road (so it wasn't actually in Sharp). Big Rocky was somewhat elusive, requiring a walk through the woods, with the mysterious trek there making it a bit more steeped in nostalgia. The general consensus is that *Little* Rocky was actually located in Sharp. It was often used in the 1950s and 60s for baptisms by both Sharp United Pentecostal Church and Sharp Church of God. It had a sandbank large enough for cars to park and a cliff for diving. It was also the site of several drunken incidents of skinny-dipping.

1957. Big Rocky. Photo courtesy of Lawrence "Buddy" Martin.

In this story, I mention Iva Martin Beebe (1914-1999) as a hallmark of the community. She truly was my "Aunt Ivy" as she was my paternal grandmother's sister, but I believe she was "Aunt Ivy" to everyone in Sharp.

Tree, Wood, Cross was written in 2013. The "seed" of the story was the real-life tragedy of a family who died in a house fire. The family lived in Grant Parish, Louisiana, and was buried in Sharp's Campbell Creek Cemetery. The story introduces 9-year-old Missy, the narrator for the entirety of this project, and gives the origination of her unique spiritual thinking.

218

Missy connects Dub's wooden crosses to "her tree" where she routinely swings in her front yard. Then, though she's not at an age where she can fully realize or articulate it yet, she finds larger meaning in seeing the crosses lined up infinitely at the cemetery.

The poignancy of a group funeral in a small, Louisiana community really touched me. I kept thinking of how such a profound loss would leave a lasting impact. Imagine the dramatic scene of five hearses in a row—an entire family gone at once. I did not know the family. In fact, I didn't even know their names. All I knew was that the name "Dub" was connected somehow.

In July 2023, as this collection began to take shape, my niece and I went to the cemetery in search of the five graves. We braced ourselves for a scorching hot afternoon, as the temperature was 105 degrees that day, and we had no idea of where the graves might be. The cemetery is quite sprawling. Yet, to our surprise, we found them immediately.

After finding the graves and discovering the name "Basco," I contacted my longtime friends, Gary and Wendy Basco, who connected me with Annette Odom Setliff, the sister of one of the deceased. Annette gave me permission to list the real names here, agreeing that it is another way to keep their memories alive.

William Mack Gore, Jr. (1969-2008)

Gleneria Ann Odom Gore (1967-2008)

William Mack Gore, III (1999-2008)

Dustin Wayne Basco (1994-2008)

Anthony David Basco (1992-2008)

Annette further explained that "Dub" is a nickname for her dad, William Moore Odom, Sr.

"Tree, Wood, Cross" is not a true representation of events and is not meant to make light of a family's tragedy. Its purpose is to emphasize the importance of finding perspective on or coming to peace with circumstances that cannot be changed. The story is a seminal part of the whole because it reveals the beginning of Missy's deep understanding of the circle of life and her sense of being OK with it all, even death.

By Any Other Name introduces Raym, who is Raymond Cupples, my dad. The nickname was given to him by his wife, Sharon. Raym absolutely adored Sharp and knew every detail of its history. He also had a knack for storytelling and a very nostalgic mindset. Ultimately, all of these stories are rooted in memories—some his, some mine.

Raym was known to be eccentric in many ways, such as his habit of using a boxcutter to cut perfectly aligned diamond shapes into the tops of his loafers "for air." His antics, though odd, were endearing, revealing his practical side along with a quirky creativity. He loved music (he could play most instruments by ear), antique cars, and literature, and he had a very tender heart. Boo Boo (introduced in the next story) really was our cat who lived to be 18 years old. After Dad died, I found an envelope in his desk with a tuft of Boo Boo's hair. He'd clipped it before burying him under the daylilies outside the kitchen window in 2011, a simple act that preserved memories, a bond that lingered long after Boo Boo was gone.

"By Any Other Name" also introduces Lah, Missy's lifelong best friend, who appears in several stories. Lah is a real person, LaDonna Graham Hargis, and I've had to ask forgiveness multiple times for incorporating her the way that I do. She's been very good-natured about it, even laughing at how some of the traits I've imposed upon her make her appear a little weird. It's a fun sort of weird though, a complete letting down of guards that comes from a very deep and enduring friendship. And, truth be told, some of the quirks are real, even if a bit outrageous. The original version of this story had Lah singing the "Boogersnot" song, a tune she made up when we were kids, and one we jokingly sing to this day. Her bond with Raym was special, and I wanted the stories to reflect the father-daughter relationship they shared.

Most readers have assumed that Missy is me, and she is somewhat an autobiographical character. However, in my mind, she's more a blend of myself and a few others, including my cousin Melissa Beebe Smith, who lived in Sharp next door to me, and my friend Sarah Kile, who I also grew up with. I chose the name Missy for the narrator because Melissa is the truest representation of the Sharp Community to me. She chose to stay and raise her family there, literally across the field from Raym's house.

Bingo and Thomas (Tut) are only loosely based on real people. My mother did sell Tupperware for many years and lots of the teasing about that is true. As Bingo is mentioned in other stories, however, the traits are not those of my mother. Finally, I do have a big brother in real life and Dad did call us Big and Little, but that's the end of any biographical references to my brother. I've largely tried to leave him out this project (though I suspect he's just as nostalgic about Sharp as I am). He still lives a few miles from there today.

Little Puppies in Heaven. There have been at least ten versions of this story. It has been 60 pages and it has been 10 pages. It's very significant to the whole—so much so, in fact, that I had planned originally for it to be the title story. Like several other stories, the idea originated from a funeral. Dad spoke at the funeral of my mischievous aunt, Mackie Cupples Guidry, who is a character in several stories. He touched me when he talked about their childhood and how Mackie explained to him what heaven would be like, saying, "there would be little puppies there." With this one simple statement, a seed was planted that grew and grew over the years (the story was first drafted in 2010). I started thinking of death in a softer, somewhat strange, but undeniably wonderful way. There's the slight feeling that the narrator is pulling the reader's leg, inviting them into a playful, but profound contemplation. It's a willing suspension of disbelief that's used for a purpose. I will confess that I do like the idea of a **congé** as portrayed here. What a fabulous way to send someone off, and to truly celebrate the continuation of life.

So many antique cars cycled through Raym's garage. He would meticulously restore one and then sell it and start another. Black and white photos do not do them justice, so for car enthusiasts, I've included photos of a few cars in my online portfolio. This Model A was memorable to me.

He had two over the years as well as a Shay Model A (a replica of the beloved model).

Donnell is not a real name in this story. Though I remember Dad mentioning a "Donnell," I have no further reference. Sarah Knight and Clovis Allen are real names, however. They were precious elderly women from Sharp Church of God (though I don't actually remember them singing). The references to Mackie and her accordion (and her enjoying drawing "little peters") are true.

So Great a Cloud of Witnesses is a story with many layers. On the surface, it centers upon three lifelong friends—Missy, Lah, and Tut—and the bonds of growing up together in a trusted place where they have no reason to question anything about life. But Tut, whose real name is Thomas, is a questioner who needs to figure things out for himself. In my mind, he is Doubting Thomas.

Beyond this story thread, I loved the idea that something was buried beneath the kids' fort that bolstered them. Something invisible that provided security and strength. In Biblical times, a foundation stone would have had a hole in its Southeast corner that led to the "well of souls." Having this in the midst of their safe place enables a sort of "knowing" for Missy. She has a sense that God is near throughout her life, but she's too young to articulate it appropriately. She just knows there's more to the creek incident than a man and a pickup where they shouldn't be.

Though it could be said that this is a story about the things we bury, my intent is to highlight the preciousness of having a sacred place to which we can perpetually return. 1 Peter 2:7 says, "Unto you which believe, it [the cornerstone] is precious." I sought to capture a specific

224

moment when the character realizes this truth. Thomas discovers something beautiful and peaceful about the baby's keepsakes being buried in *their* fort, by *their* creek, and, in that moment, he understands that Jesus has been walking beside him his whole life.

High Potential is a nod to my dad's years as a notary public and justice of the peace. The anecdotes in the story are fictional; however, there were many similar incidents in real life. Families would come by not just for the notarization of documents, but for him to settle a feud. It was nothing to see two brothers out in the front yard, standing at odds facing each other, slowly begin to hang their heads as he spoke to them. His tone was gentle and understanding, but it carried a weight that made people recognize their actions were foolish. He especially enjoyed performing marriages, and there were plenty of them in the kitchen or on the front porch. Among the files I discovered in his desk after his death was a listing of 566 couples he'd married.

The Great Schism is about a split that actually occurred within the Sharp United Pentecostal Church in 1952, though my rendition of it is largely fictionalized. It's the longest piece in the collection because it's written from Dad's notes and stories passed down. While the full scope of the argument is unknown, after the split had been decided, it was reluctantly agreed that both factions would temporarily share the church building. In the stifling Louisiana summer heat, when all the windows were open during a service and when tempers were  already stretched thin due to the disappointing decision to split, my uncle, Burel Cupples, who would've been 12 at the time, dove into the church through one of the open windows to attack a boy whose parents were on "the other side," inciting a brawl. At left is a photo of Burel Cupples from 1946.

Both sides supported the idea of physically moving the building. However, it could not be done without cutting the limbs of trees which belonged to a member of the other sect. The deacons had to beat down the tin roof as it was being moved. An entire story could focus on the fascinating way the church was rolled out on logs.

The details of Sister Melba singing and playing her guitar were also in Dad's notes. He wrote that her husband overheard the comment, "You thank she's 'bout to yodel, babe?" This started a confrontation in the parking lot. The true last name is unknown. The notes only refer to "Sis. Melba." Some have suggested to me her identity, but I have been unable to locate her family or confirm it. The story is only meant to be humorous and not to slight a real Sister Melba.

226

It probably goes without saying that music in a Pentecostal church service was taken very seriously. The information about the Kimball organ is mostly accurate as the church did obtain an impressive new model, and part of the schism was indeed related to a long-running feud over who played the piano and organ.

According to Dad's notes, my Aunt Mackie was involved in the contest in real life, and it resulted in the family of the other musician moving to another church. Mackie, as I've expressed repeatedly, was mischievous and enjoyed throwing runs of "carnal" songs into the music, especially during times when the "praying and seeking" was at a climax. Dad lived for these moments of the service. I can just see Mackie squinching her nose at him when she'd do it, and the two of them cutting eyes at each other every time she got away with it.

1949. Raym and Mackie.

My story was getting long so I didn't include this, but one other interesting detail is that, after the church was moved, a "Bro. Earl" and my grandfather, George Cupples, fenced up the end of a dirt road so that no cars could enter. Even though several members of the other faction lived down this road, Brother Earl owned the land on both sides. He'd knowingly cut off access to their homes. Brother Earl and Brother George, in essence, fenced up a public road. A lawsuit was filed, and the fence had to be removed.

Finally, while most names in this story are fictional, Sherman Martin was actually a deacon at the Sharp Church of God where we attended when I was young. I used his name in early versions of this story because I always thought of him fondly. I've kept it here, even though it wasn't his church, simply because his family has enjoyed that I mentioned him.

1947. A few women of Sharp UPC. Left to right: Willie Mae Riggs, Velvie Hodges Rice, Temone Martin Cupples, Grace Allen.

1949. Men of the Sharp UPC. Left to right: Charlie Beebe, Layo Cupples, Joe Carter, Hesicar Fay, Bill Murphy, Earl Riggs, Oliver Allen, George Cupples, Mack Sterling, Hershel Lee Handly, Allen Martin, Earnest Riggs.

1958. Temone Martin Cupples, Willie Mae Riggs, Essie Mae Beebe, and Maxine "Mackie" Cupples.

1946. Members of Sharp United Pentecostal Church. This photo shows the symmetrical windows and the blocks supporting the building, making it easy to be moved in the manner described in the story.

1944. George and Temone Cupples (at left) with a Sunday School group outside the Sharp UPC.

1951. George and Temone Cupples with children Mackie, Burel, Tommy, and Raymond at the approximate time of the church split.

MOIALT (My Once in a Lifetime) was written to honor my aunt, Maxine "Mackie" Cupples Guidry, who died after battling cancer. As with other stories, there is a seed of truth. What Mackie says about not being scared and the minister praying for her wig were actually courageous words spoken by my friend Cynthia Pinchback Gossett (1969-2022) the day before she died.

I had been captivated for years by the intriguing inscription on Mackie's headstone: MOIALT. It's a romantic inscription; however, as I was crafting the story, the depth of the acronym began to come alive to me in new and unexpected ways. I had the realization that Missy, our narrator, ultimately has the same plight in nearly every story—she's searching for things that are authentic and meaningful. Mackie was authentic, of course, which is why I loved her so much. Missy's ongoing search for a genuine religious experience works well in tandem with the story of Mackie's death.

2000. Mackie Cupples Guidry (1935-2002).

Marianne Moore, a modern poet I studied in depth in graduate school, has a poem simply entitled "Poetry." She writes: "I, too, dislike it: there are things more important than all this fiddle. / Reading it, however, with a perfect contempt for it, one discovers in it, after all, a place for the genuine." Perhaps this helps explain why Missy suddenly looks at the preacher and despises him. She shuns any sort of rote language or pageantry, and she has the feeling that he's said the same prayer over so many sick people that there's no meaning to the experience. Instead of the preacher, she finds what she's looking for in the elderly doctor (the great physician) who gently assists her through Mackie's final moments. It's a heavy-handed metaphor as Jesus is often referred to as "the Great Physician."

I wanted this story to be funny because Mackie was so very funny. My first draft included the lyrics to Walt Mills' "Devil's in the Phone Booth (dialing 911)" instead of Connie Smith's "I Wouldn't Take Nothing for My Journey Now." In the end, it was important to choose a song that Mackie would've actually sung.

Secession is focused on the characters finding the courage they need to launch a personal revolt against the heavy weight of social and religious expectations. Boon, the hound dog, was Ms. Donnie's constant companion, and, even when he dies right in front of her, she still has the remarkable deportment to graciously invite guests into her home for iced tea. After taking a moment to digest what has happened and how she wants to handle the situation, she finds clarity and realizes that it's perfectly OK to be vulnerable, to step outside of the stereotypical mode of expected Southern hospitality and decorum. Only then does she truly become her authentic, spiritual self. It's when Ms. Donnie breaks that she shows her true humanity—it's also when she feels the love of Jesus, her bridegroom, most. In a parallel journey, Missy and her students, belonging to generations that question everything, embark on their own search for truth. They find liberation and experience a breakthrough when they recognize that, just like Hunter, it's within their power to evoke meaningful change in the world.

When I was very young, we lived on the Lena Road in Flatwoods, and there was a real Ms. Donnie (Donnie Hillman) that lived "up the lane" from us. I saw a dog get killed in this exact manner and never forgot it. While I was horrified, no one said a word about it. I am a huge animal lover, and the way in which Ms. Donnie and Bingo respond in the story is unfathomable to me.

In addition to Donnie Hillman (and her husband Bob), the other names in the story are true as well. Ella Mae Watkins Hillman (and her husband Duffie) lived next door to us in the early 1970s, and they lived next door to Ella Mae's mother, Sarah Martin Watkins, who was 102 years old when she died. Ms. Watkins' great granddaughter, Sarah Kile, has been one of my lifelong friends.

The Shivaree is based on an actual incident of good-natured hazing by grandchildren and friends when Sybil Knight Martin (1894-1971), my great grandmother, married Elias Beebe (1887-1969) in 1940. Sybil was 46 and Elias was 53, and both of their first spouses were deceased. I'd heard about the shivaree from several sources, all with differing details, except for consistency in the fact that the shivaree ended when Elias came out onto the front porch firing his shotgun into the air.

1940. Sybil Knight Martin and Elias Beebe. Photo courtesy of Sybil's granddaughter, Arleen Sybil Aucoin Hague.

For years, I thought Dad had participated in this event, but after digging into historical facts, I learned that it was before he was born. I've left the date of the shivaree out of the story, mainly for this reason. In truth, the date became problematic in many ways, and "The Shivaree" has gradually become a story about stories and what we get out of them, especially in the retelling of them. The only sure facts are that the "old shiv" happened at some point while the "new shiv" is completely contrived (although Raym did give Lah away

at her wedding in real life). Lah, LaDonna Graham Hargis, seen here in a photo from 2022, is frequently exasperated by gullible people who ask about her cemetery wedding, even though it's as fictional as her "floppy toe" (a topic she is frequently asked about as well).

The text messages that I include are verbatim texts from Dad that I've saved and cherish. Additional stories could easily be written from some of his other messages, which capture his fascinating knowledge of history and

the interesting context he enjoyed adding. At left is a photo of Rudolph "Sonny" Barker (1931-2012), my uncle, from during his time in military service in the U.S. Army from 1951 to 1953, during the Korean war.   Just a few years later, Tommy Cupples would go on to serve honorably in the U.S. Air Force from 1957 to 1961.

236

I sought facts for this story from both Buddy Martin and my "Uncle Tommy" (Thomas Cupples) to try to make the "old shiv" incident as accurate and vibrant as possible. Uncle Tommy or "OTom" as he's known by his grandchildren, remembers climbing in through a window and unlocking the door for everyone, and Buddy remembers Elias and the shotgun. However, when I obtained the marriage license for Sybil and Elias via the Louisiana Clerk of Court's office, the marriage was in

1940—the year Buddy was born and Uncle Tommy was three years old. Some have suggested that the shivaree actually occurred years after the wedding as a playful act of hazing instead of a celebration on the honeymoon night while others have said that it's a tall tale that's gained a life of its own through the years. In reality, the truth doesn't matter. At left are the most representative photos that I could find of Raym (top) and Tommy (bottom) to convey how I visualize them in the story. All names in this story are real with most of the "band of brothers" being cousins.

Raym and OTom shared a deep passion for antique cars. In their later years, they worked on many projects together, complementing each other's expertise. To accompany this story, here's "the bean." Photos of this car in color, as well as a couple of Uncle Tommy's cars, are found in my online portfolio.

1960 Chevrolet Impala (aka "the big green lima bean").

Finding these next two photos, despite their poor quality, was a real treasure. Both are perfect representations of the truck I envisioned in the story.

"Big Boy." A 1947 Studebaker pickup that Raym purchased from Harlis Beebe for $35 and then sold to someone else for $20 and a 16-gauge shotgun.

238

1955. My grandfather's 1955 Ford, parked in front of the Cupples' home with the store in the background.

Showdown at Victory FBC is a story I wrote in 2015 that was originally entitled "The Kiss." I did not pick it up again (or rename it) until 2024. As a writer, I'm never satisfied, but there are elements in this story that work well, so I didn't want to revise it. The narrator is trying to find something that will bring her out of a state of ennui. She's become very jaded with life, and especially religion or religious rituals (as highlighted in "MOIALT"). She's left her career as a professor to be a reporter, and now she's jaded by this role as well.

As a reporter, she witnesses a family's intense pain when the wayward son comes to the funeral, and she realizes that this—the pain—*is* the story. It also wakes her up. For a moment, she feels a connection, a glimmer of true humanity that she'd long forgotten. Yet no sooner has the realization settled in, than doubt creeps back, and she undercuts her awakening when, in the last line, she thinks, "It changed my life forever. I just know it did." Here, I think the reader knows better, and that any new understanding she has found will only be temporary. Her cycle of cynicism, even in the face of revelation, speaks to a deeper spiritual restlessness she hasn't yet resolved.

The seed idea for this story came from the funeral of my grandmother, Temone Martin Cupples, when I was a senior in high school. At the end of the funeral, when those in attendance were asked to file by the casket in the traditional manner, Dad stopped and kissed his mother on the cheek. It was a simple gesture, but it stuck with me for years. The pain in that one moment is hard to articulate, but I think that kiss said it all.

Fierce Like an Oak Tree is an autobiographical story about the day I unexpectedly lost Raym, and, just a few hours later, had an appointment to check a suspicious new mass following two years of intense breast cancer treatments. Writing it was my way of processing life events that felt unjust because they happened at the same time. I realize that life isn't paced via an invisible counter where a bad morning guarantees a good afternoon. I also realize that cancer recurring in the breast area after a double mastectomy is exceptionally rare. Still, something in me wanted to vent about feeling like I had been sucker-punched by that day's events, and to share the thought process of finding strength again afterwards.

240

Most of the details in this story are true. After writing it, I called Peggy Newburn to ask permission to use her real name, and we talked about how I put on a smile and acted like everything was fine when I saw her that day. It's just one more aspect of Southern life that fascinates me—the notion of pleasant small talk, even when emotions run deep beneath the surface. Dr. Tyler Leete was also incredibly kind (and humorous) throughout my treatments, so I asked permission to use his name as well.

I mention Little Eva Plantation in both "Secession" and this story. When I taught college English in the late 1990s, it was common to take students on field trips to the Kate Chopin house (also known as the Bayou Folk Museum) and Little Eva, both located in Cloutierville, with a final stop at Lasyone's in Natchitoches for a meat pie. The Kate Chopin house, built by slave labor in the early 1800s, became the home of the author after her marriage, inspiring her most famous work, *The Awakening*. It's tragic that the house was destroyed by fire in 2008, as it stood as an important representation of Louisiana heritage.

The trees at Little Eva, along with the history behind the plantation, have always charmed me. As a character, Eva embodies a veiled strength that I aspire to possess. And the trees are simply majestic. Their perfect rows, equally spaced, convey a sense of forethought and order that is a perfect metaphor in this story. Their longevity, too, speaks to endurance and resilience.

The full history of Little Eva, including notes about the connection to folk artist Clementine Hunter, can be found at natchitochespecans.com.

Even though the circumstances conveyed in the story are difficult, the narrator gradually understands that everything happens in God's time, as if part of a checklist, allowing her to walk through life at peace. Her steps are ordered. This is my story told through Missy's voice. However, the real-life Missy, Melissa Beebe  Smith, shown here, also had a difficult experience that I could have used to express this same journey as she lost her husband to COVID in 2020, becoming a widow at 48. In the end, for both of us, I wanted to conclude the series by leaving readers with a tone of growth, acceptance, and quiet strength.

Some might wonder why I didn't title this story, and the entire collection, *FAITH Like an Oak Tree.* I hope the element of strong faith has been evident. To me, the word "fierce" puts a bit more roar behind the metaphor, if you will, while also implying that the faith is steadfast. To stick with some of the Southern war jargon I've used in various stories, perhaps I envision a good rebel yell while charging into battle, all the while knowing victory is sure.

Those who started at the beginning and read through to the end will recognize that this story brings the narrative full circle back to the oak trees in the front yard of my childhood home in Sharp. It was bittersweet when, in September 2023, my brother and I sold the homeplace. It felt right though, as we sold it to a couple with deep family roots in the community. Also, years before, Raym had married them there in the living room.

A few weeks after the family moved in, I received a text from Wendy Randall Basco, who drove by and saw that children were playing in the front yard. She wrote, "I think the trees are smiling." For me, that's enough.

2023. Raymond Cupples' home in Sharp.

Additional photos can be found at raecuppleschampagne.com.